"You can't  to you," Keith said.

"Cancer's terminal," she told him, trembling as she spoke.

"*Life's* terminal," he said. "You've never had a relapse, never had a problem."

"Neither had you," she countered.

"You can't measure yours by mine. Where's that 'never give up' attitude you're so famous for?"

"Maybe I'm just tired of the whole mess. Maybe I'm sick and tired of watching my friends suffer. It's like we hurt and hurt, and there's no way out of it. The doctors can't help us. Mommies can't kiss us and make us well. God won't do a miracle. What's left?"

He laced his fingers through hers. "Just because this is happening to me now, there's no reason for you to think it's going to be the same way for you. We all aren't asked to die when we're sixteen."

Other Bantam Starfire Books you will enjoy

NOW I LAY ME DOWN TO SLEEP

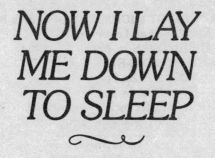

Lurlene McDaniel

BANTAM BOOKS
NEW YORK • TORONTO • LONDON • SYDNEY • AUCKLAND

RL 5, age 10 and up

NOW I LAY ME DOWN TO SLEEP
A Bantam Book / April 1991

*Bantam Books are published by Bantam Books, a division of Bantam
Doubleday Dell Publishing Group, Inc. Its trademark, consisting of
the words "Bantam Books" and the portrayal of a rooster, is Regis-
tered in U.S. Patent and Trademark Office and in other countries.
Marca Registrada. Bantam Books, 666 Fifth Avenue, New York, New
York 10103.*

I would like to thank Judy Whedbee and Hospice of Chattanooga. Thanks also to Valerie Blancett and Joel Alsup, who live with cancer every day.

Now I lay me down to sleep,
I pray Thee Lord my soul to keep.
If I should die before I wake,
I pray Thee Lord my soul to take.
—CHILDHOOD PRAYER

Chapter One

"But Mom, you *told* me you'd take me for my bloodwork today," Carrie Blake said as she stood in the doorway of her mother's bedroom.

"I know, honey, and I'm sorry I have to back out. But my boss wants me at a meeting this afternoon with one of our biggest clients. I just can't pass up an opportunity like this." Faye Blake scurried around the room dressing as she spoke. "Besides, it's not like you've never gone to the clinic alone before. You've been going for six months—it should be routine by now."

Carrie felt resentful. How could she explain her fear that her bloodwork would be abnormal? And that being alone during her clinic visits was getting to be a drag? "Yeah, it's pretty routine all right," she mumbled. What other ninth-grade girls at Martin High School have such a normal routine of checking for a relapse into leukemia?

Her mother sat on the bed and gathered her pantyhose. "Look, if it's bothering you that much, call your father. Have him come get you. He should be helping me out more anyway."

Carrie didn't want her mom to get off on *that*

topic. "When we talked on the phone last night, he said they'd be pouring cement today, and you know he can't leave the project till that's done."

Mrs. Blake tugged the hose to her waist. "So ask his new wife. Maybe Lynda can pick you up."

"She can't. Bobby's got a Little League play-off game at four."

Mrs. Blake slumped. "I forgot—now I'm going to miss that too." She turned toward Carrie, her brown eyes clouding. "Do you really think he understands, Carrie? He's only nine, but he *did* want to live with your dad. I just don't want him to think I abandoned him, you know?"

Carrie sighed. "He's doing great, Mom."

"Last year it seemed like the best thing to do when I went back to work. Besides, Lynda doesn't work, so Bobby doesn't have to go to day care like he would if he lived here with us."

Carrie had heard her mother rationalize her choices hundreds of times. Her mother kept asking her kids to forgive her for divorcing their father, and Carrie kept feeding her the reassurances she wanted to hear. "You see him every weekend, Mom. He's used to it."

"Maybe we swap you kids around too much," her mother said.

Carrie almost blurted, *But it's what you wanted.* Instead she changed the subject. "Look, don't worry about my clinic visit. I was just being a baby about it."

At her dresser Mrs. Blake rummaged through her jewelry box. "Carrie, this is the easy part. That first year—with the diagnosis and all—and then the chemo and remission . . . well, this part seems like a piece of cake. I really think you've beat your disease, Carrie."

Your disease, her mother always said. To her it would forever be Carrie's problem. Throughout her hospitalization and clinic treatments, her parents fought over it. Whenever her father confronted his wife about not staying with Carrie in the hospital, her mother had argued, "There's an entire staff to take care of her, Stan. What can I do to help?"

And her father would shout back, "For crying out loud, Faye, you're her mother, and she's just a twelve-year-old kid. Stay with her!"

And then her mother would yell, "Why don't *you* spend your day up there? You know I can't stand hospitals and needles and those tests that hurt her—why aren't you holding her hand while they stick a foot-long needle into her spinal column? She's so sick afterwards. I hate it!"

"I work, Faye," her father would yell back. "She needs her mother!"

And her mother would yell, "Well I'd work too, if you'd let me! But no, you have some pigheaded idea that I need to be home all the time."

"Your place is with your family!" he'd shout.

Finally it got so bad that Carrie simply ignored them and asked her doctors and nurses to explain the procedures to her. Carrie realized that she knew more about her leukemia and its treatment than both her parents put together, and watching her mother prepare for work made her painfully aware that she probably always would. "Well, I guess I'd better take off, or I'll be late for school. I'll catch the bus to the hospital after school and then home after I'm finished." One advantage to living in a city the size of Cincinnati was its convenient transportation system. On her way out she asked, "What's for supper?"

"Oh, Carrie, I'll be going out to dinner with Larry Farrell. You remember meeting him?"

"The man from your office," Carrie said matter-of-factly. "Gray suit, white shirt, and wing tips. A real catch." Not like her father, who smelled of sweat and construction dust, she thought.

"A brilliant CPA," Mrs. Blake added sharply. "He's been a big help with my clients' accounts. And he's nice too. Goodness knows I need a nice man in my life after all the years I put up with your father."

"So is there something in the fridge for me if you and Larry go out to dinner?" Carrie asked quickly.

"Some leftover meat loaf. And there's a pizza in the freezer."

Carrie's stomach reacted to both suggestions. "Maybe I'll grab something at the hospital after I finish in the clinic."

Her mother made a face. "How can you even think about eating that disgusting hospital food if you don't have to?"

"It's not so bad."

"I'd think you'd have gotten your fill of that place. I hope I never see the inside of that hospital again."

Carrie had felt the same way, at first. But a person

didn't spend three years of her life as she had without feeling some sort of kinship with the people who'd helped her through it. "I think Hella's in the clinic today. Maybe she'll grab a bite with me." At the mention of her favorite nurse, Carrie smiled. If it hadn't been for Hella, there'd be no teen support group, and without support group—

"Maybe she'll give you a lift home. I'm not crazy about you riding the bus after dark."

But not bothered enough to change your plans, Carrie thought. She watched her mother fluff her hair, remembering when she'd been only a housewife and her father was the one stumbling around the bedroom getting ready for work. Bobby had been in the second grade, and she'd been in chemo, still trying to go to school even though she was vomiting most mornings. They all lived together in the same house and at least pretended to be a family. "So I hope your meeting goes well," Carrie said.

"Thanks," Mrs. Blake answered. "Carrie, you *do* understand about my not being able to take you, don't you?"

Carrie looked at her mother, at the stylish blouse and new-wave haircut, pearl earrings and expensive heels. "It's no big deal, Mom. Like you said, it's routine for me."

Mrs. Blake smiled her approval and finished doing her hair.

Chapter Two

~

"We're almost finished," the lab technician said.

Carrie watched in bored fascination as the clear glass vial, attached to the syringe stuck in her vein, filled with her blood. She guessed that she'd given them an ocean of blood during the length of her illness.

"Sticking you kids is always the worst part for me," the tech said.

"It beats the catheter," Carrie told him. "Or taking it out of the neck like Count Dracula." She arched her eyebrows suggestively and made him laugh.

She hated wearing the Hickman catheter, but the apparatus made it easier for patients to receive chemo. Nurses would simply hook the IV tubing attached to the bag of chemo medication to the small IV tube inserted beneath her shoulder blade that led to a vein deep in her chest, and the solution would drip inside her. It saved getting stuck hundreds of times and her veins from collapsing. Still, the device had been a nuisance, always needing to be flushed and cleaned. And even though no one could see it, sometimes it got hung up on her bra, and without warning a bright red spot of blood would appear on her shirt.

"Have you seen Hella Smithe today?" she asked the tech.

"She was in the chemo room about an hour ago." He slipped the needle out of Carrie's arm and taped a cotton ball to the puncture. She automatically crooked her arm, holding it tightly, so that the bleeding would stop and a bulge wouldn't form in the vein.

She left the lab and walked through the clinic, passing through areas that were now as familiar to her as her own house. In the chemo room Hella was hunched over a small boy stretched out in one of the contour chairs used during chemotherapy. Carrie said, "I'll hold her off, and you make a run for it, kid."

The boy giggled and Hella turned. "I thought I saw your name on the schedule. Wait just a minute and I'll be with you."

Minutes later Carrie found herself with Hella in the nurses' lounge sipping a cola. "Are you coming to support group Friday night?" the blond-haired nurse asked.

"Don't I always?"

"Is it because you have such a swell time talking about cancer, or could it be because of Keith Gardner?" The nurse's voice held a teasing tone.

Carrie felt color creep up her neck. "Maybe a little of both. It helps to talk about it."

"So how are things at home?" Hella asked.

Carrie found Hella's sensitivity amazing. She always seemed to know when Carrie was upset or down. Maybe it was because she'd worked so hard with Carrie's parents about accepting her diagnosis and treatment without blaming each other. Hella also knew that Carrie's home life was something she'd never discuss in the group. "Mom's really crazy about her job and some guy in her life. I think he's sort of a dweeb, but my opinion doesn't count for much with her."

"What are your summer plans?"

"Find a job, I guess. I can't work full-time till I'm sixteen, but even part-time would help."

"Don't forget the support-group picnic on Memorial Day."

"How can I? I'm in charge of games."

Hella fiddled with a paper napkin. "I was thinking I might ask Keith to help you."

"Don't you dare!" Carrie said.

"Why not? He's one of the nicest guys I've ever met, and I know he wants to help. Besides, he's cute."

"You know why not," Carrie told her.

"Because you think he's cute too and would rather *die* than let him know it?"

Carrie tried to act casual. "He doesn't even know I'm alive."

"Of course he does. I noticed him watching you at the meetings."

"You'd say anything to make me agree to one of your plans."

"Well, you need help with the games, and it's either Keith or Sharon Haverly."

Carrie groaned and dropped her forehead against the tabletop. "Not Sharon. That girl never stops talking."

"Name your poison," Hella said coyly.

"Some choice! Either I drown in Sharon's nonstop blabbering or in my own nervous perspiration."

"Yeah, isn't love the pits?"

"I don't *love* him, Hella. What do I know about love? I've spent the past three years learning about cancer."

Hella patted Carrie's arm. "Then it's about time you learned that they can both leave you nauseous."

"What a comforting thought," Carrie mumbled, her mind already racing in anticipation of Friday night.

Carrie stood at the refreshment table in the front of the hospital auditorium trying not to stare at Keith Gardner. But like a magnet her eyes kept finding him. She knew that Keith had once had Hodgkin's disease, that he was sixteen, an athlete, a sophomore at Martin High, and probably the most gorgeous male she'd ever set eyes on. Why had she ever let Hella talk her into pairing them on the picnic-games committee?

She chose a chocolate-chip cookie from a tray and dipped herself a ladle of raspberry punch. Some prankster had hung a sign on the bowl that read: "This is NOT adriamycin"—the name of a drug commonly used in chemotherapy that caused nausea. She smiled at the inside joke, glad that chemo was behind her.

"Hella tells me we're doing a committee thing," Keith said.

"That's what she told me too. Do you mind?"

"Not if you have any good ideas."

"I don't have a single one," she admitted, making him laugh.

"Well, according to Hella this picnic's going to last from noon till dusk, so we'd better come up with something."

"Baseball's good," she said quickly, because she knew his sport was baseball. "Adults against us."

He surveyed the room, which was rapidly filling for the meeting. And because it was the only adolescent cancer support group within a fifty-mile radius of Cincinnati, the room was already crowded. Girls, bald from chemo and wearing hats, scarves, and wigs, boys with crutches, and teens with artificial limbs were taking seats in the small theater. "It hardly seems like a fair matchup to me," Keith said. "We'd kill 'em."

Carrie giggled. "Probably. But what's a picnic without a ball game?"

"How about tug-of-war?"

Carrie watched one boy balance a small bucket on his lap and knew at once he'd been to chemo recently and therefore might start vomiting at any moment. "Only if we do it over a mud pit. Wouldn't you love to see Dr. Fineman in the mud?" She named an oncology specialist popular with the kids.

Keith nodded. "And a three-legged race? How about that?"

Carrie saw another boy unstrap his artificial leg and prop it against the seat beside him to save a place for a friend. She looked back at Keith. "Unfair advantage for our side. They'd cry foul."

Keith laughed again, and she noticed how his

green eyes sparkled. "We're going to have fun planning these games, Carrie." She hoped her nervousness wasn't showing. "Why don't we get together after the meeting and talk some more?" he asked.

"Uh—no, not tonight." Lynda, her stepmom, was picking her up to take her to her father's for the weekend. "Other plans," Carrie finished lamely.

"How about tomorrow then? It's Saturday. I could drive to your house. Don't you live near the high school?"

She wondered how he knew where she lived. She'd still be at her father's, so she suggested, "How about we meet at the library?"

"Sure. I'd have never thought to meet there."

"I used the library a lot when I was in and out of the hospital so much. The librarians were real helpful and would let me check out any books I wanted because I was too sick from chemo to get to most of my classes."

"The library it is. What time?"

Carrie could hardly believe he was making a "date" with her. "Is ten o'clock all right? I'll wait for you on the steps."

"See you tomorrow." He waved and headed up the auditorium steps to the upper gallery. The rim of overhead lights left the top part of the room edged in shadow, and she watched until Keith disappeared from view.

Chapter Three

"How was your meeting?" Lynda asked as she maneuvered her car through the late-night traffic.

"Pretty good," Carrie answered, without looking over at her.

"Are you hungry? We could stop at McDonald's. Or how about the Donut Shop?"

"We had punch and cookies at the meeting."

An awkward silence fell. Carrie sat still, torn between feeling sorry for her stepmother, yet resenting her too. Maybe if Lynda hadn't come along so soon after her parent's divorce, they might have gotten back together. Carrie glanced at Lynda. She was a petite woman, younger than her mother, pretty in a natural outdoorsy way, with curly brown hair and brown eyes.

At first Carrie had tried to dislike her, but she honestly couldn't. Lynda chauffeured her on weekends, bought her gifts for "no reason," and sometimes slipped Carrie money for clothes. Carrie wondered if Lynda ever regretted taking on her father's two kids— especially a kid with cancer. Occasionally she asked Carrie questions about her disease, but mostly she didn't pry.

"Bobby wanted to come with me, but I talked

him into waiting at home on the sofa. I'm sure he'll be asleep when we get there, but wake him up. He really wants to see you tonight," Lynda said, breaking the silence.

"When's Mom getting him?"

"She's supposed to pick him up tomorrow after Little League practice."

"Um—I have to meet someone at the library tomorrow. Could you drop me off when you take Bobby to practice?"

"Of course. Will you need a ride home?"

"I'm not sure. Can I call you? I'm supposed to meet with a guy from the support group to plan the games for the Memorial Day picnic. It may take most of tomorrow." Carrie hoped so. She'd rather spend the day with Keith than hang around her dad and stepmom all day. "Don't worry about me if you want to do something. I can catch the bus home."

"Your father wouldn't hear of it."

"I'm not a kid," Carrie said defensively, and later at the house, after she'd hugged her dad and kissed a sleepy Bobby good night, her father told her the same thing. "I don't want you riding city buses," he said, his face a scowl.

"I do it all the time."

"When? You live less than six blocks from school."

"I took the bus just the other day to get my blood-work done at the lab."

"What!" her father's fist hammered the kitchen table. "Your mother put you on a bus to go to the clinic? That's a forty-five-minute ride through a bad section of town. What's the matter with her? Couldn't she leave her precious job long enough to take you for your bloodwork?"

Nervously Carrie shuffled her feet under the table. She should have known better than to have mentioned it. Her parents had never agreed on how to raise their kids and had fought about it often. "Dad, it's no big deal—"

"That woman is irresponsible."

"She's busy with her job." Carrie wanted to defend her mother.

"'Busy.' She was always busy with everything except what's important."

Lynda interrupted. "Stan, it's history, and it's late. I'm sure Carrie would like to go to bed."

Carrie flashed her a grateful look. "Sure," her father said gruffly. Carrie stood and started past him. He reached out and put his arm around her waist, and the gesture of affection surprised her. "I just worry about you, that's all, and I like having you here. I miss you, baby."

"I miss you too, Daddy." She hugged him back and then hurried up the stairs to her room. The house was new and smelled of fresh paint, and it wasn't at all like the house where she'd grown up and now lived with her mother. Suddenly she missed her house and wished that her parents were still living there together, despite the arguing. One thing was for sure in Carrie's mind. Loving families were only to be found on TV shows, not in real life. She was *never* going to fall in love. Never.

*   *   *

The next morning Carrie had Lynda drop her at the library early, where she waited on the steps for Keith. The day was mild and bright with sunshine, and the air smelled of May flowers. She was watching the fluffy clouds float past, wondering if they might taste like cotton candy, when Keith bounded up the steps.

"Hope it's this nice for our picnic," he said.

"We could look in the *Farmer's Almanac* and see what they forecast."

"Do you learn *everything* from books?" he joked. "Some things are better learned firsthand, I think."

She blushed. "Not everything," she said. "I—I just like books, that's all. Reading's fun."

"Books are all right. But give me real life anytime. And the great outdoors," he added.

"I like being outside."

"Do you like to camp?"

"Do you?"

"Man, my family camps all the time. We have this cabin in the Carolina mountains near a lake, and we go there for a month every summer."

"I thought camping was done in tents."

"You've never seen this cabin. When we first bought it, we had to pump drinking water and build a fire for the wood stove so that Mom could cook and light oil lamps at night."

"Hunt your own game too, Daniel Boone?"

Keith laughed. "Are you saying I'm boring you?"

He could read the phone book to her, and she

wouldn't be bored. "No, I just can't imagine being without electricity and—" Her eyes grew wide. "What about bathrooms?"

"There was an outhouse out back," he said with a grin.

She couldn't imagine such a thing. "How many in your family?"

"Six."

"Your mother cooked on a wood stove for seven people?"

"We have electricity now and running water. But there's still plenty to do, so we all pitch in. My sister Holly's fourteen, and she and Dad and I do the heavy stuff. My other sisters, April and Gwen—they're eleven and eight—are born campers, and even Jake, who's five, helps out."

"What can a five-year-old do?"

"He gathers kindling for firewood and sorts the laundry."

"Do you beat it on rocks in the lake on wash day?"

His green eyes sparkled with mischief. "Actually we pile it in the van and drive it down the mountain to the laundromat." He leaned closer. "And while we're in town, we take in one of them newfangled picture shows."

"You're teasing me." She grinned good-naturedly. "So, are you going up there this summer?"

His smile faded. "It depends."

"On what?"

"On how my cancer's doing."

Reality, Carrie thought. "You have Hodgkin's, don't you?"

"Yeah, since I was nine. I responded really good to the initial treatments, and things were fine until I was thirteen and it flared up again. I had more treatments and was given a clean slate. Then a couple of months ago, I started feeling dragged out, tired all the time. Dr. Fineman said I was anemic, and he's been treating me for it."

"But it isn't a relapse?"

"No. I feel better now, and that's good, because I was worthless on the pitcher's mound until they got my red blood count up."

"Martin's baseball team *is* hot this year."

His eyes lit up once more. "We're smokin'! In fact, some colleges are scouting me already."

"Is that what you want to do? Play baseball?"

"Why not? Do you know the kind of money those guys make?"

"Lots."

"What do you want to be?" He didn't wait for her answer. "A librarian?"

"I want to rule the world," she said sweetly. "And if I do, I *might* let you have your own baseball team."

"Why thanks, Carrie. I'm touched." They laughed together. "Maybe we'd better get started on this picnic project," he said.

They entered the library, where she felt at home. She quickly found books full of game ideas and made a list.

"Here's something they play in India with live snakes," Keith whispered.

She stared at the page. "That's disgusting."

"All right, how about this one from Fiji? All we need are a couple of coconuts."

"Will you be serious," she said, without meaning it. She scanned the list. "Besides, I think we have enough."

"Don't you think we'll have to get together again before the big day?"

Her heart began to pound, and her mouth went dry. "If you like."

His eyes bore into hers. "I like," he said. She felt her cheeks grow scarlet, but if he noticed, he didn't say anything. "So let's blow this joint. We've been sitting here for an hour, and I'm getting claustrophobic. I need to be outside," he said.

On the way to the door, Carrie stopped and pulled the *Farmer's Almanac* from the shelf. "It says here that Memorial Day will be sunny and dry."

"You believe everything you read in books?"

"Do you have to experience something before you believe it?" she countered.

They stepped into the warm sunshine. He told her, "I like being in control of my life. That's why I like being a pitcher instead of a catcher, or an outfielder. A pitcher controls the game by the way he throws the ball."

Carrie's problem was that she had no control over her life. She got cancer with no warning. Her parents divorced without asking her permission. She had two houses, but no real home. But Keith had cancer too, and he'd had no choice about it either. "Sometimes we don't get to decide what happens to us," she said after they'd settled beneath a tree.

"All the more reason to control the things we can," he told her. "I'm still planning to go to college and play ball—cancer or not."

"But what if it comes back?"

"I'll make it through somehow. And my family will be there for me."

He made his family sound like superhumans, like seven people who actually wanted to be together. He'd probably made them up. "Will they be at the picnic?"

"You bet. We do everything together." His inflection had said, *What family doesn't?*

She asked, "Your sisters too?"

"They're pretty neat—for girls."

"I'll tell them you said so."

His expression grew serious. "I have a great family, Carrie. We stick together, but our parents have always urged us to think for ourselves and to make our own decisions."

She couldn't imagine such a thing. Her parents had fought about everything, and so she'd learned to make decisions by default. A horn honked, and Carrie looked up to see Lynda waving her toward the car.

"Who's that?" Keith asked.

"My stepmom," she said with much embarrassment. With all the talk about ideal families, what would he think about hers?

Keith followed her to the car, where she leaned down to see Bobby's dusty, tearstained face. "What's wrong?" Carrie cried.

"Mom forgot me!" Bobby blurted.

Lynda said, "Now Bobby, I'm sure your mother will have a good explanation." She said to Carrie, "His coach called me from the field. Evidently your mother never showed. I'm sorry to bother you, but he's pretty upset, and he wanted to see you. Do you know why she didn't make it?"

Carrie felt her cheeks burning, not only from anger over seeing Bobby so distressed, but at having Keith hearing the whole incident. "No," she said miserably.

"Will you come home, Carrie?" Bobby asked.

"I'd better go," she told Keith, barely able to look him in the face.

He opened the door, and she slid inside. Keith asked Bobby, "You coming to our picnic?" Bobby shrugged. "If you do, maybe you could show me your fastball."

Carrie looked at him gratefully. "I'll call you," he said. She was so engrossed in soothing her brother that she was almost back to her father's house before it dawned on her that Keith Gardner—the most popular sophomore boy at Martin High—had actually promised to call.

Chapter Four

"I told you! That piece of junk that passes for a car broke down, and I was stranded!" Faye Blake yelled.

"And there wasn't a phone anywhere around?" Stan Blake yelled back.

"And who was I supposed to call? The Little League dugout? There's no phone at the field, and you know it."

"You could have called Lynda."

"Well, as it turned out, Bobby's coach called her, so what's the problem?"

Carrie was holding her breath while her parents stood in the kitchen of her mother's house screaming at one another. Couldn't these two *ever* talk to each other? Why did every encounter end up in a yelling match?

"The problem is, the kid was scared to death! What's he supposed to think when his own mother forgets him?"

"I explained things to Bobby, and *he* understands. You're the one who won't leave it alone, Stan."

Carrie went out onto the front porch and sat on the stoop. She'd heard enough. More than enough. She was positive that even though her parents were divorced, they'd never stop hating each other. She pressed her face against her drawn-up knees, and sighed. Finally she heard the back door slam and her father's car drive away. Minutes later her mother came and sat next to her on the stoop.

"You understand, don't you, Carrie?" she asked.

"Yes, Mom."

"I would never have 'forgotten' Bobby."

"I know, Mom." Truthfully she didn't know. Her mom was a stranger to her since she'd started her "new" life.

"Stan wants you to live with him and Lynda, you know."

Carrie jerked her head up. "What?"

Her mother turned her head, but not before Carrie saw moisture brimming in her eyes. "He thinks I'm incompetent."

"That's not true!" Carrie felt her stomach knotting.

"He says he's worried that I can't take care of you properly."

"You are taking care of me, Mom."

"You know that I work hard to give us a good life."

Carrie twisted her hands. "Dad works hard too."

"He has no idea what it's like trying to get back into the work force and still be a real mother. Before I had you kids, I had such a wonderful job. Now I'm starting from scratch. Bobby must hate me."

"No he doesn't. He's just confused, that's all."

"Lynda is good to him, isn't she?"

Carrie nodded. She wanted to say that Lynda was

a nice woman, but she wasn't sure her mother wanted to hear it. "You've got me," she said.

"You won't leave me, will you, Carrie?" Carrie wasn't sure what she meant.

"I live with you, Mom. I won't leave."

"Larry says that I should start thinking about myself and what I want because you kids will be growing up and starting your own lives someday."

The mention of Larry bothered Carrie. She wasn't nuts about the guy, but he did make her mother happy. "What do you want, Mom?"

Mrs. Blake closed her eyes and leaned against the sagging porch railing. "I want to succeed in my job. I want to travel and dress pretty and be with exciting people."

Carrie wondered where she fit into such a scenario. Especially if she got sick again. "Well, I don't know about dressing pretty," she said, attempting to lighten the mood. "But there'll be plenty of exciting people and travel to an exotic park by the river for the support group's Memorial Day picnic. We'll have fun."

Her mother touched Carrie's shoulder. "I—uh— I've been meaning to talk to you about that, dear."

"What about it? You *are* coming, aren't you? Dad won't be there, and Bobby and I want you to take us."

"There's a convention in Orlando, Florida, and Larry thinks it's a good opportunity for both of us to go. Sort of a working vacation, you know."

Carrie felt dismayed. "But I thought the picnic was something we could do as a family."

"Honey, put yourself in my place. This is a wonderful chance for me to impress my boss. I may not get it again. Tell me you understand."

Carrie felt a salty sting in her eyes, so she turned her head. "It's not important," she finally said. "It's just a stupid picnic and nothing but warm food and a bunch of dumb games."

Her mother put her arm around Carrie's shoulders. "Thanks for understanding. Larry and I'll bring you and Bobby some souvenirs from Disney World. All right?"

Carrie only nodded, because she couldn't trust her voice. Her mother went inside to start dinner, and Carrie wrapped her arms around herself and watched until the sun set and the stars began to come out.

Keith spoke to her whenever she passed him in the halls at school. It made her feel wonderful and impressed her friends too. "A fringe benefit from having cancer," she told one friend, who made a face and said, "No thanks."

He asked to take her home after the next support-group meeting. "We can stop for a hamburger if you want." She wanted to more than anything, but she was sure her father wouldn't let her. She called from an auditorium pay phone and broached the subject with Lynda. "Do you want to go?" Lynda asked.

"A whole bunch," she admitted.

"Then go. I'll handle your father."

Carrie was momentarily speechless. "You'd do that for me?"

"Just be home by eleven. And have fun," Lynda told her.

Carrie went with Keith to his car, hardly believing her good fortune. He opened the door as she asked, "What kind of a car is this?"

"A fifty-seven Chevy. My dad's a car buff, and we restored this one together. It's neat, huh?"

She ran her palm over the dashboard. "It's different from the new ones."

"Next to baseball it's my one true love."

"Besides gym what class do you like best?" Carrie asked.

"Promise you won't laugh?"

"On my honor."

"I like music. I play guitar."

"So?"

"Not rock stuff. Classical."

"Who'd laugh about that?"

"It's not macho."

She let out a moan. "That is so juvenile! Will you play for me sometime?"

"If you want. Do you play anything?"

"The radio," she confessed, and he laughed.

"You're funny, Carrie."

"That's what Hella says too." She didn't want him to know that she used humor to cover up her fear. "Someday I'm going to do a stand-up routine about cancer."

"Like what?"

"What's soft and white and covered with hair?" she asked.

"I give up."

"Your pillow after two weeks of chemo."

Keith groaned.

"Why did Dracula ignore the boy with cancer?" She didn't wait for his answer, saying, "Bad blood between them."

This time Keith chuckled. "Okay, so you can go on Johnny Carson and warm up the audience before I come on and wow them with my music."

At the hamburger place they ordered only milk shakes and shared a plate of fries. "My stomach's been bugging me," Keith said, when she told him that he wasn't eating his share.

"You're still pitching for our side at the picnic aren't you?"

"You bet. Tonight at the meeting Dr. Fineman was bragging that he'd hit a homer off me."

"Well, we certainly can't let him get away with *that*," Carrie announced, thumping the table.

Keith asked, "Do you and Bobby want a ride to the park? I thought we'd better get there early to help set up."

"That would be nice," she said calmly, afraid of sounding too anxious. "My mom's out of town, and my dad's never liked hanging around all this cancer stuff. Lynda was going to drop us off."

Keith broke into a smile. "Then no problem. I'll pick you up and bring you home afterwards."

She nodded, self-conscious about making it

sound as if no one in her family cared about the event. Deep down she knew that Lynda would have come if her father could have been persuaded. But he'd never participated in anything having to do with the hospital. Even when she'd been first diagnosed and he'd visit her on the oncology floor he'd stand fidgeting at her bedside, and leave as quickly as possible. He'd told her, "I got my fill of sickness and death in Vietnam. You just get better, baby, and come home quick."

Unfortunately, her mother hated hospitals too. No matter now, she thought. All that was behind her. She looked across the Formica table at Keith. "Thanks for the offer. Without Dad to control him, Bobby may act wild."

"No problem. My sisters can handle him."

"They'd do that?"

"In my family it's all for one and one for all."

Carrie almost blurted, "In mine it's every man for himself." Instead, she shoved a french fry into her mouth and told him, "Tell your sisters they're on, and don't forget your guitar. I want to hear if your playing is as good as my stand-up material. I don't plan to go on national TV with just anyone."

Chapter Five

The morning air smelled sweet, like new-mown grass mixed with honeysuckle and lilies. The cerulean blue sky had changed to a bright, vivid hue of cornflower by the time Carrie, Keith, and Bobby arrived at the covered pavilion in the park. Members of the hospital staff were already setting up tables for food, and washtubs of ice for drinks and watermelons, and had started a charcoal fire in the massive stone grill.

When they found Hella, she said, "It's about time some of the guests arrived. Got those games organized?"

Carrie set a bowl of Lynda's potato salad on one of the tables. "We have to fill the water balloons, but that won't take long. Did you get the pillow cases for the sack races?"

Hella glanced about with a conspiratorial expression. "Don't let anyone from housekeeping hear you ask that. They'll have my head." She scurried off to help set up the food table.

"Don't you love the smell of the outdoors?" Keith asked, closing his eyes and inhaling. "There's nothing better to me."

"How about charcoal-broiled hamburgers?"

He shook his head. "Not even close."

Carrie had never been one to love the outdoors, but seeing Keith's enjoyment added to hers. People began to converge on the pavilion. He pointed toward a very tall, slim blond man and a short, plump black-haired woman. "There're my folks. Come meet them." He grabbed her hand. "Hey, Mom, Dad!"

Carrie met his parents, Gwen, April, and Jake. "Where's Holly?" Keith asked.

"Still bringing food," his father said.

Keith eyed the table already heaped with two ice chests and a wicker basket. "Cripes, Ma, there's enough here to feed a small country."

His mother patted his hand. "Don't be silly. It's better to have too much than not enough."

His father hugged his wife's shoulders. "We certainly don't want anyone to go home hungry, do we?"

Carrie noticed that Keith's brother and sisters had brown eyes like their father, but Keith's brilliant green eyes were the same color as his mother's. Mrs. Gardner studied her son. "I brought extra because you didn't eat any breakfast."

Keith shrugged. "I wasn't hungry."

April squealed, "You're *always* hungry."

Keith tugged on her ponytail. "Make yourself useful, short stuff. Carrie's brother Bobby is around here someplace. Take Jake and Gwen and go find him. You have to get ready for the relay races."

Carrie expected the girls to complain, but they agreed willingly. "He's wearing a red T-shirt and a Dodgers baseball cap," she said. They ran off, almost colliding with another girl who she knew at once was Holly. She resembled Keith but had brown eyes and light brown hair.

Holly set down a large chocolate sheet cake. "So you're Carrie."

"Guilty," Carrie said.

"Watch out," Keith told her. "She's about to bombard you with nosy questions."

Holly stuck out her tongue. "Just mildly curious, that's all. Like what's a nice girl like you doing with a geek like my brother?"

Keith chuckled. "The CIA is only mildly curious compared to my sister."

"Oh, shut up," Holly said, grinning. Carrie realized that they probably always teased one another that way. She turned to Holly. "Ask me anything you want to know."

Holly peeked around her toward her brother. "Is it true what Keith says about his being able to do better in the three-legged race tied to a tree than to either one of us?"

"He said that?"

"Scout's honor." Holly looked the picture of innocence.

"She lies like a rug!" Keith protested.

Carrie ignored him. "I think we should make him eat his words, Holly—and our dust."

"Is that a challenge?" asked Keith. The other kids ran up, with Bobby in tow. "How'd you like to run in the three-legged race with me, kid?"

Bobby agreed instantly, and in minutes Keith had

grabbed Dr. Fineman's bullhorn and announced the first event. At the starting line Holly asked Carrie, "Have you ever done this before?"

"Nope."

"Neither have I."

They burst out laughing and at the blast of the whistle started for the finish line at the far end of the field. They fell three times, got turned around once, and were laughing so hard by the end of the race that they could scarcely stand. Keith helped untie their legs saying. "At least Bobby and I won our heat."

"We'll do better in the water-balloon toss," Carrie assured him. An hour later they had won that event. Dr. Fineman announced that the burgers were ready on the grill, so Carrie lined up behind Keith, heaped her plate from the food tables, and followed him to a blanket spread under a tree where his family had gathered. Midway through the meal Gwen handed Keith his guitar, and he played songs that people could sing. As she watched him play, Carrie decided that Keith made everything fun.

Finally he called the concert quits and whispered, "Let's go for a walk."

"How about the ball game?"

"In an hour."

He slung the guitar over his shoulder, and they started down a winding trail through the park's woods. The sounds of the picnic faded, and the noise of humming insects and crunching leaves took over. She watched sun-dappled patterns play across his hair and shoulders while the heavy woodsy scent smelled sweeter than any perfume.

The air grew thick, damp, and humid. Keith stopped and sniffed deeply. "It's going to rain," he told her.

"No way. The *Farmer's Almanac* said—"

"Who are you gonna believe? Me—the great outdoorsman—or some silly old book?" He took her hand. "We'd better find some shelter, or we're gonna get drenched." The sun vanished, and a breeze stirred the leaves. It felt cool, and even she could smell the moisture. Keith spotted a rock overhang and stooped beneath it, pulling Carrie and the guitar behind him. The shelter was deeper than Carrie had first thought, but low. She sat, Indian style, and rested her back along the smooth, cool granite.

Thunder clapped and rain came down in huge, fat drops. "It wasn't supposed to do this," she told Keith in exasperation. He'd pulled his guitar across his lap and was plucking at the strings.

"I think you should sue the publishers of that almanac," Keith said. The notes he chose were beautiful, haunting, and she told him so. "Classical Spanish guitar is my favorite," he said. The melody was so pretty that Carrie's eyes filled with tears. "What's wrong?" Keith asked.

"Nothing. It just sounds so sad."

"Lonely," he countered. "To me it sounds lonely."

"When did you learn to play?"

"During my second round of chemo and radiation. It was a bad time for me. I thought I had the disease licked. When it came back, I felt sort of betrayed. I got really bummed out. Then one day my dad brought me this guitar. He never let me give up when I was trying to learn to play it, even when my fingertips got raw from the strings."

"It hurts to play?"

He held up his hand where she saw calluses on the ends of his fingers. "Until the calluses form, you hurt." He pulled plaintive notes from the instrument. "And as I got the hang of this guitar, a funny thing happened inside me. I started caring about getting well. If it hadn't been for my dad . . ." He let the sentence trail.

Carrie hugged her knees. "You have a nice family, Keith. I really like them."

"Thanks. Your stepmom seems okay. I'll bet you've got a good family too."

"I have parents," she said wistfully. "Not a family."

She was grateful that he didn't ask any questions about them. "My mom gets a little fanatical about food sometimes," he said, "but she was there for me during every treatment, every blood test, every spinal tap." He leaned toward Carrie. "At one point she got it into her head that maybe I'd respond better to the treatments if I ate health foods. Man, she had the whole family chowing down on brown rice, tofu, and bean sprouts. We almost starved to death. Holly used to hide Twinkies in her room, and late at night we'd pig out."

Carrie laughed. "It wasn't that way for me," she

said. "My parents were blown away when the doctors told them I had leukemia. My dad could hardly look at me. My mom hung around for a while, but the hospital gave her the creeps, and then she and Dad were having problems between them."

Carrie stared into the rain. The air had turned cooler, and she shivered. "I was lucky because I responded well to the induction phase of chemo and went into remission. 'Course I still had to do maintenance for two years, but now"—she shrugged—"now all they do is keep tabs on my bloodwork and hope that it never comes back. I—I don't want to go through it all again."

She didn't know how to tell him that she didn't want to do *any* of it again. Not just the chemo, but the family breakup either.

"I guess that's why I hate being anemic," Keith said, setting his guitar against the stone wall. "It makes me worry that the cancer's coming back. There's so much I want to do."

"Like play baseball and the Johnny Carson show?"

A smile turned up the corner of his mouth. "I never used to think about living long. I'd see an old guy and think, 'Hurry up, old man.' Now I think, 'It must be good to have your joints ache because they're old and not because they're eaten up with cancer.'"

Carrie listened to the rain, to its slowing rhythm. She plucked one of the guitar's strings. "Could you teach me to play?"

"Would you like to learn?"

"Yes," she said.

His green eyes were bright, like the color of new spring leaves. He ran his knuckles along her cheek gently, and her heart fairly leapt into her throat. "I'll teach you," he said. "I'll teach you whatever you want to know."

Chapter Six

The rain stopped, and the sun broke out from behind its prison of clouds. Keith put the guitar strap over his shoulder and helped Carrie crawl from under the overhang. Keith inhaled, saying, "Just smell that air, Carrie."

She closed her eyes and sniffed the aromas of wet grass, rich, damp earth, and moist, clean air. She would never have noticed their distinct and separate fragrances if he hadn't been with her, and she wondered how the world could seem more colorful, more sweet-scented whenever she was with Keith. "Yes, Nature Boy," she joked, because her feelings were making her embarrassed. "Maybe we should all live in tree houses and drink rainwater."

"Just for that wisecrack we're gonna do the tug-of-war right over the biggest mud puddle I can find. But first, I think we should get the baseball game under way."

When they got back to the picnic area, Keith grabbed the megaphone and said, "All right everyone! I want to see your faces at the baseball diamond. We have a game to play!"

Carrie and Holly decided to escape before the game started, to use the park rest room.

"You get along pretty good with your brother," Carrie said, once they were inside. "You seem to really care about each other."

"We're all pretty close. Keith's the oldest, and we've always sort of looked up to him. When he went in the hospital the first time, I was only seven, and we'd had a fight the day before. You know, I thought it was my fault that he got cancer."

Carrie wondered what Bobby had been told when she'd been diagnosed. Until now she hadn't considered what he might have been thinking and feeling. "Come to think of it, Bobby got tummy aches whenever I went for chemo."

"So did April. Every time Keith got sick from the drugs, she'd be right in the bathroom barfing alongside him."

Carrie shuddered. "I still hate to go into the chemo room at the clinic, because I know how sick you can get after the treatments."

"Keith says that all that's behind you now."

Carrie nodded. "Forever, I hope."

"The second time Keith went into the hospital was worse," Holly confessed. "I was eleven then, and I'd done a lot of reading about cancer, so I knew more. I was so scared for him."

"He told me that he got pretty depressed the second time."

"Yeah, it was a bad time for the whole family. I

think because we really believed that he was going to be one of the lucky ones who beat the statistics, and then suddenly, BAM!—he's right back where he started from."

Carrie washed her hands and doused her face with cool water as Holly talked. "It was worse for him too because he was thirteen and had a crush on this girl named Amanda."

The mention of a girlfriend made Carrie's mouth go dry. Holly continued. "She was the prettiest girl in the middle school. They were both eighth-graders, and everyone thought they were so cool together. But then Keith got sick. You know, she never once called him or came to see him. He got so bummed out about it. He got behind in his schoolwork too. Keith's always had to study extra hard to make good grades, but he couldn't concentrate. It was all Amanda's fault. If only she'd stood by him."

Holly paused, then said, "Later I found out that Amanda dropped my brother because her parents made her. They were afraid she'd catch cancer from him. Wasn't that dumb? Everybody knows you can't *catch* it."

Carrie remembered how her friends had treated her at the time. Many had stayed away from her, acted snobby. Now she wondered if they had thought the same thing. "I guess that's why I like support group so much," she told Holly. "Everybody understands what you're going through, but they don't treat you like you're gonna break either."

"Hey, that's what Keith says. Are the two of you friends at school or just in support group?"

"He says hello when he sees me in the halls, but us lowly freshmen don't mingle much with sophomores."

"Well, next year I'll be a freshman at Martin. Will you mingle with me?"

Carrie couldn't help but grin. "Sure I will, Holly." And she meant it. "We'd better hurry up—wouldn't want to miss that ball game."

At the baseball diamond teams were being chosen and positions assigned. This time Carrie and Holly both ended up on Keith's team. He sent Carrie to left field and his sister to first base. "What about me?" Bobby asked.

"Shortstop," Keith told him.

Moments later Carrie stood in the outfield watching Keith deliver his famous fastball to a hapless batter, who struck out quickly. Yet when a ten-year-old girl with a leg brace came to the plate, he walked her. One of the radiologists stepped to the plate. Keith licked his fingers, tugged at the bill of his cap, and wound up for his pitch.

Carrie saw the ball leave his hand. She heard the bat crack against it, saw the ball head straight toward the pitcher's mound and strike Keith hard in the shoulder. She heard Keith's wail of pain and saw him collapse onto the dirt mound like a broken doll.

Chapter Seven

In seconds the mound was swarming with people. Carrie raced forward too but couldn't get close. She heard Dr. Fineman yell, "Get back, all of you."

Carrie strained to see through the press of bodies. Holly grabbed her arm. "Can you see? What's happened to my brother?"

"It's his shoulder," a voice announced. "I think it's dislocated. Let's get him to the hospital."

The crowd stepped backward, and Carrie saw several people lift Keith and start across the field. Keith's moans made her sick to her stomach. "Holly!" Mr. Gardner shouted. "Come on! Your mom and the others are already on the way to the van."

Carrie watched helplessly as Holly ran ahead of her dad. She felt a tug on her hand and looked down to see an ashen-faced Bobby. "Will Keith be all right?"

She could scarcely control the tremble in her voice when she answered. "I think so. There're plenty of doctors to help him." She wanted to go to the hospital too. She wanted to be close by when Dr. Fineman reported to Keith's family in the emergency room. From the corner of her eye, she saw Hella heading toward the parking lot. "Hella! Wait! Are you going to the hospital?"

The nurse turned. "Yes."

"Please take us with you."

"It could be a long wait."

"I'll call Lynda, and she can come get Bobby, but I want to be there. I *have* to be there."

They rode to the hospital without saying much, and once there Hella led the way to the emergency-room waiting area. When Holly saw Carrie and Bobby, she said, "Oh, Carrie! We haven't heard a thing yet."

Mr. Gardner was holding his wife's hand and was telling them, "It's a sports injury. A bad one, but these things happen."

Still, they all looked frightened. "But he *always* pitches, and he never gets hurt," April cried.

Hella disappeared into the ER, and Carrie hoped she'd soon be back with some kind of report. She searched her pocket for a quarter for the pay phone but ended up borrowing one from Mr. Gardner. Shakily she dialed her father's number and explained the situation to Lynda. "I'll be right there," her step-mom said. When Lynda arrived, Carrie introduced her to Keith's family, who promised to get Carrie home safely. Before Lynda left with Bobby, she slipped Carrie ten dollars.

"What's that for?" Carrie asked in surprise.

"In case you want to get something to eat."

Carrie was touched by Lynda's thoughtfulness. A

part of her longed to have her mother there, but of course she was in Florida, and besides, she wouldn't be there because she hated hospitals. Holly interrupted her thoughts with, "What's taking so long?"

"I don't know."

"You don't suppose he's really hurt bad, do you?" Holly twisted her hands together while she spoke. "This isn't right. It's not fair."

The doors from the patient area of the emergency room slid open, and Dr. Fineman emerged. His expression looked set and businesslike. He shook Mr. Gardner's hand, and Carrie edged in closer, feeling like an intruder, but wanting to be a part of the group.

"His shoulder was dislocated," Dr. Fineman said. "I put it back into place and called in an orthopedist. We X-rayed, and the film showed plenty of tissue trauma."

"How is he?" Mrs. Gardner asked. "Can we take him home?"

Dr. Fineman adjusted his glasses. Carrie noticed that he still wore mud-caked sneakers, and there was a smudge of dried dirt along his receding hairline. "I want to keep him a few days for observation."

"But why?"

"In the routine exam I gave him on the table, I felt a slight enlargement in his abdomen I want to check out."

Carrie saw Mrs. Gardner slip her hand into her husband's. "What does that mean?"

"I want to run some tests."

Carrie backed away, because she didn't want to listen anymore. She kept seeing her parents' faces when a doctor had told them she had to be checked into the hospital for tests. Her mother had clamped her hand across her mouth, and her father had slammed his beefy fist violently against a nearby wall and shouted, "I want my little girl out of this place!"

"What do you want us to do?" Mr. Gardner was asking.

"I'm sending him up to oncology. It's the floor he knows best, and I think he'll be more comfortable up there. You can all go up in about fifteen minutes and say good night to him."

"Me too?" Jake asked in his little-boy voice.

Dr. Fineman crouched in front of him. "You too. I'll tell the staff you have my permission."

Twenty minutes later all of them were standing around Keith's bed. Carrie felt a sense of déjà vu being on the oncology floor. "Hey, buddy," she heard Mr. Gardner say. "How're you doing?"

Keith lay with his shoulder wrapped, his mouth set in a grim line. "I want to go home, Dad."

"It's just for a few days, son."

"But I've got baseball district-finals and final exams coming up."

Mr. Gardner shook his head and said gently, "The season's over for you, Keith. You know that."

Carrie saw Keith squeeze his eyes shut and wad up the sheets with his fist. "This stinks."

"I'll get in touch with your coach," his dad said.

"And I'll talk to your teachers," his mother quickly added. "I'm sure we can work something out."

"I want to pass, Mom. Not like last time. I want to stay with my class."

"Rest right now, and we'll be back in the morning. Things always look better in the sunlight."

"Yeah, sure." He sounded so despondent that Carrie felt a lump in her throat.

Holly leaned over the bed. "Do you want me to bring anything from home?"

"My Walkman and some of my tapes. You know which ones."

Carrie waited while each family member bent over and kissed Keith; then she stepped forward. "Is there anything you want me to tell the kids at school?"

"Tell them to stay away. I'll be home in a few days."

"Even me?"

For the first time he offered a slight smile. "You can come visit if this place doesn't give you the willies."

"You mean the Little Shop of Horrors?" She used the name kids in support group had tagged the oncology floor. "I'm a veteran, remember?"

He smiled again, and it made her feel good. "Thanks, Carrie."

Later, during the ride to her dad's house, Mrs. Gardner said, "Whenever you want to visit Keith, please call us. We'll be glad to pick you up and bring you along."

Carrie thanked them. Next to her Holly whispered, "I'm glad we're all friends, Carrie. This time Keith won't feel so all alone." Carrie nodded, but she knew that as long as Keith had his family around him, he would never be alone. And she hoped he would never know what it felt like to have anything less.

Lynda and her father were sitting at the kitchen table drinking coffee when she arrived. She told them what had happened, what Dr. Fineman had said, and how much she wanted to be at the hospital for as long as Keith was a patient. "You've hardly been here all weekend," her father grumbled. "And you go back to your mother's tomorrow night. I've hardly had any time with you at all."

"But Daddy—"

Lynda broke in. "Now, Stan, we've been through this. Carrie should be with her friend if she wants."

Stan Blake shrugged his shoulders in resignation. "I know, I know. Look, I'll pick you up from school, and we'll all have dinner together. Then I'll drop you off for visiting hours. We should at least all eat together."

"Sure," Carrie said. "And Keith's parents can take me back to Mom's tomorrow evening. Her plane gets in at six o'clock." Wearily she sat at the table and started talking about the picnic, adding, "We could have used you in the tug-of-war, Dad." She knew she sounded piqued but couldn't help it. Why was he not there for her when it mattered, yet he made such a big deal over eating dinner together?

"I thought your mother was going to go to the picnic."

"She had to change her plans, but you could have come."

"Look, you know I don't like being around all those poor kids."

"But this was a picnic, not the hospital. We were all having fun."

Her father stood abruptly. "Things just got fouled up this time. Next time we'll all do your picnic together, if your mother lets me know in advance that she can't take you." He told Lynda, "I'm wiped out. I'm going to bed now."

"Why does he make it out to be Mom's fault?" Carrie fumed, once he'd left. "He just doesn't care about the things that are important to me."

"It's hard for him to show his feelings, Carrie," Lynda said.

Carrie wanted to shout, *What would you know! You're not part of our family! You weren't there when I was all alone in the hospital*. "Keith's dad shows his feelings," she said.

"Your father's different. He cares, but it's hard for him to show it."

"Well, pretending something isn't wrong won't make it go away."

Lynda reached out and touched Carrie's arm. "We know that, but he doesn't. It's just his way of coping."

Carrie jerked back her arm and stood. "All I know is that my friend is in the hospital, and something more's wrong than a hurt shoulder. I'm going to spend every minute I can with him. And Dad had better let

me, because people stand by people when they care."
She spun and hurried to the door. Lynda called her
name, but Carrie ignored her, rushing up the stairs
and throwing herself across the bed, where she wept
for Keith, for herself, and for the terrible, aching lone-
liness that chewed away at her insides.

Chapter Eight

~

"You know, Carrie, I thought you'd be more enthusiastic about the things I brought you from Disney World," Faye said as she unpacked her suitcase.

Carrie stared down at the Mickey Mouse beach towel, the Cinderella jewelry box, and the hat with mouse ears. Didn't her mother realize that she was too old for a stupid mouse hat? And Cinderella—what girl her age still thought about Cinderella?

"I dragged Larry from shop to shop so that I could buy you and Bobby gifts."

"How nice of him to tag along."

"Don't be sarcastic. Larry is a wonderful man, and he really likes me."

Carrie bit her tongue. Her mother sounded juvenile, like a lovesick seventh-grader. Frankly, Carrie wasn't interested in the particulars of her mother's relationship. "I told you, Mom, it's hard to be excited about anything with Keith in the hospital."

"And it's hard for me to come back full of excitement and see you so down in the dumps."

Carrie sighed and scooped up her presents. "I'd better go to bed. You remember that I'm catching the city bus tomorrow after school and going straight to the hospital."

"Yes, you already told me." Faye shook out a skirt. "How long will you be doing this?"

"For as long as Keith's in the hospital."

"What about your homework?"

"I can handle it, and anyway, there's only a few weeks of school left."

"Carrie, I don't mean to be insensitive, but hanging around the hospital . . . well, it isn't emotionally healthy."

"He's my *friend*, Mom, and I know how it feels to be alone with nothing to do but watch TV and not have anyone around to talk to all day long."

She saw her mother's hands pause. "I was with you as much as I could be," she said quietly.

"I didn't say you weren't. I just said that the days get long. The nurses on the floor are busy, so you sometimes have to spend a lot of time by yourself. I figure that I can help Keith not to be so bored."

"Well, don't make plans for Thursday. I've asked Larry to have dinner with us. I think it's time the two of you got better acquainted."

"I don't know how late I'll be at the hospital," she hedged.

"You can skip one visit, Carrie. It's important to me for the three of us to eat together. I ask very little of you, you know. And while I'm thinking about it, we need to discuss what you'll be doing this summer."

"I was planning to get a job."

"I think you should. My paycheck never seems to go far enough, and your dad's no help." She glanced around the room and gestured toward the windows. "This place is falling apart. It needs all new screens before summer, and the water heater's older than Noah's ark."

"Maybe Dad—"

"He was always too busy to fix it up when we were married, so I doubt he'll get to it now. Meanwhile he sits in a fancy new house while this one's falling down around us."

"It's not so fancy," Carrie said defensively. "It's just newer."

"Right," her mother said with sarcasm. "Anyway, if you want new clothes for school next year, you're going to have to earn the money to buy them."

Carrie said good night, and once in her bedroom she tossed the beach towel and mouse ears into her closet and stuck the pink-and-white jewelry box on the back corner of her dresser. How could her mother buy her such childish gifts and then turn around and tell her she was grown-up enough to get a job and buy her own clothes? It made no sense to Carrie. No sense at all.

Outside Keith's hospital door the next afternoon, Carrie squared her shoulders and pasted on a big smile before she breezed into his room, saying, "So, hotshot, how do ya feel?"

A grin lit up his face. "Like a pin cushion. Thanks

for coming. I was beginning to think I'd have to face this *Gilligan's Island* rerun alone."

He clicked off the TV set as she pulled a chair next to his bed. "Tell me about it," she said.

"Bloodwork today." He held out his arm, crisscrossed with tape inside his elbow. "Tomorrow they're doing a colonoscopy—some sort of medieval torture that includes a needle biopsy of my intestines."

Carrie made a face. "That doesn't sound like much fun."

"Yeah, but that's the fastest way to find out what's going on inside my guts."

He looked so dejected that Carrie wanted to cry. Instead she told him, "No blue funks allowed. If you're interested, you were the talk of the school today."

"What'd they say?"

"Mostly wailing in the halls because you won't be pitching in the districts for Martin."

Keith sighed. "Coach was up here at seven-thirty this morning checking on me. I really hate letting the team down."

"How's the shoulder?"

"Sore."

"So you wouldn't be pitching even if this other stuff hadn't come up."

He shook his head. "I told Coach we'd get 'em next year."

For the first time Carrie noticed books heaped on the nightstand. "Homework?" she asked.

"Yeah. Mom talked to my teachers this morning and brought books and assignments at lunch."

Carrie made a face. "Aren't moms thoughtful?"

He didn't smile. "The problem is, I don't think I can keep up. Especially if they put me back onto chemo."

"There's no reason to think that anything serious is wrong. Maybe you have an ulcer or something."

Keith gave her a long, level look. "Let's not kid ourselves, Carrie. I've been down this road before, remember?"

"Well, even if they do start chemo again, you can still finish the term."

"School's not that easy for me." He looked away as he told her. "I'm sort of a slow reader, and I never do good on tests. I'm already dreading the PSATs in the fall."

Carrie pulled his English text from the stack. "Making decent grades isn't so tough. You just need a little push, that's all. English is my best subject."

"And my worst."

She thumbed through the pages. "I could help you," she added cautiously.

"Help me?"

"You know, sort of tutor you. If we work together, I'll bet you can do pretty well on your finals."

"I don't know."

"What's the big deal? I'd like to help. I made the dean's list last grading period."

"I know you're smart, Carrie, it's just—uncool, you know?"

She understood instantly. She was only a freshman, and he didn't want to be embarrassed in front of his friends. Inspiration struck her suddenly. "I didn't say I'd do it for nothing."

"You'd charge me?"

"Didn't you tell me you'd teach me to play the guitar?"

"Yeah, but—"

"So that's what I'd like you to do. And I'll help you through the end of the school term. And if anyone asks, we'll just say you're giving me music lessons."

"Learning classical guitar isn't easy."

"But I'll have a good teacher."

He looked at her for a long moment before saying, "I'm game."

"So am I. Now, who's on first?"

"Correct."

"What?"

"What's on second."

They broke out laughing together. "You know that old Abbott and Costello comedy routine?" Carrie asked.

"I know everything there is to know about baseball. How do you know it?"

"I told you, comedy's my specialty. I watched lots of TV reruns when I was in treatment, and the old comedy shows were my favorites."

"So TV and books got you through. What about your family?"

Carrie sobered. "What about them?"

"When I hurt really bad, my family tried to distract me. We played a hundred board games and thousands of hands of cards. Holly and I got pretty good at double solitaire, and the whole bunch of us played Uno because it was something Jake could play too."

Carrie diverted her gaze. "We never did things like that. My parents didn't handle my cancer too well, and besides, they were miserable with each other most of the time. They split right after I achieved remission."

"Bummer," Keith said, and she could tell by the way he shifted that he was feeling embarrassed.

"Anyway, that's all over with now. Dad's remarried, and Mom's dating some suit from her office. They're both happy."

"Are you happy?" Keith ventured.

"Don't I look happy?" She smiled broadly and crossed her eyes for effect.

"You look dorky," he joked.

"Thanks a lot!"

Keith smoothed his hand over his bedcovers. "Were you serious about helping me out with my schoolwork?"

"You bet."

"Then it's a deal. You help me get through finals, and I'll teach you how to play the guitar."

His parents came into the room just then along with Dr. Fineman. "We'll be taking you down for a biopsy first thing in the morning," Dr. Fineman said.

Carrie studied his face as he spoke and noticed

that his expression was professional and clinical, not at all like the silly one he'd worn at the picnic. She'd seen the look before. Her parents had worn it the night they'd told her they were divorcing, the same night her childhood had ended. It was a look that said, "Stay back," and it made one's eyes appear guarded, as if to seal off feelings too volatile to control, and to hold back secrets too terrible to share.

Chapter Nine

Carrie didn't go to the hospital Thursday because Holly told her the biopsy had left Keith groggy, and Dr. Fineman wanted Keith to sleep it off. She felt at loose ends the entire afternoon and would have stayed in her room reading if Larry hadn't been coming for supper. She watched her mother zip around the kitchen in a frenzy, acting as if royalty was arriving. Carrie set the table and made the salad while listening to her mother rattle on about Larry until she thought she'd scream.

When Mr. Wonderful did arrive, she saw how he contrasted with her father. He was slim, blond, and impeccably groomed, yet she wondered why he'd never married and had kids. He acted polite and attentive, but Carrie couldn't change her original impression of Larry Farrell as dull and boring.

"Your mother tells me that you're quite a good student, Carrie," Larry said. "You're almost a sophomore, aren't you?"

"Yes."

"Have you thought about where you might apply to college?"

College? She'd barely thought past the end of the term. "No, not yet."

"You should be giving it plenty of thought. Top colleges fill up quickly."

"I'll keep that in mind."

Her mother flashed her a warning glance that said, *Don't be rude.* "You'll have to excuse Carrie. She's usually much more talkative, but one of her friends is in the hospital, and I'm sure that's on her mind."

"Nothing serious, I hope," Larry said.

Just life and death, Carrie thought. She said, "The doctors are doing some tests."

"I've been telling your mother that she needs to consider some investments so that she can contribute toward your future and her retirement," Larry said, as if Carrie hadn't spoken at all. "Everyone needs a nest egg, and saving even a hundred dollars a month can add up over time." He'd cut his meat into small, neat squares and was now methodically slicing his potato.

"Let's see," he mused. "You're fifteen now, and say you begin college in September, three years from now. That's approximately thirty-nine months, and at one hundred a month, why that would be close to four thousand dollars saved." He smiled at Faye. "That plus federal assistance would give Carrie a good start toward a top-notch education."

"Of course, you're right, Larry," Mrs. Blake bubbled. "It's hard, though, on my salary to think about saving."

He cut himself a pat of butter and lay it directly in the center of the steaming potato. "Yes, but you've got a bright future at the firm, and I'm sure Carrie will be working soon. That money can be set aside."

Carrie deliberately mashed her potato into a pulp with the back of her fork and smeared it with butter and sour cream. "I was hoping to get my own car," she said. "Plus I buy my own clothes."

"You'd have to weigh all the options," he said. "A car would cost in upkeep and increase insurance rates. Still, they aren't as high for female drivers under twenty-five as for males."

Carrie willed butter to drip on his spotless tie. Her mother said, "I agree that saving is an excellent idea, Larry, but it's so difficult."

He glanced thoughtfully around the room. "You own your own home, and that's an asset. It seems like quite a large house though. How much room can two females living alone really need?"

"I grew up here," Carrie said, following the path of his gaze. "This is my home."

"Yes, of course, but in three years you'll be gone, and then what's your mother to do? She doesn't need to be a slave to a place like this."

"Oh, Larry," Faye sighed. "You're so practical."

Carrie felt like clamping her hands over her ears and screaming, "Stop it! Both of you shut up." Yet it was Larry who spoke first. "One can't get attached to objects and possessions, Faye. Possessions are assets and emotions are liabilities when it comes to the things we own."

Carrie stood, folded her napkin, and placed it beside her plate. "I have a big test tomorrow. Mom, I really should go study for it."

Mrs. Blake stared at her in surprise. "But we haven't had dessert."

Larry nodded agreeably. "Let her study, Faye. You should be glad she's so responsible. My sister's girl hasn't cracked a book in two years of high school."

Carrie escaped the dining room and sat on the top landing of the staircase in the dark. She hugged her knees and listened to the clink of silver and china and low voices. She felt like crying but wasn't sure why. Maybe because Larry Farrell was such an idiot. Maybe because of Keith. Maybe because nothing was the same in her life anymore.

On Friday Dr. Fineman decided to run more tests, so Carrie couldn't see Keith then, either. She spent the night at her father's, determined to see him on Saturday. She shuffled downstairs to the kitchen close to noon and found Lynda sorting through a pile of coupons. "Where's Dad?" Carrie asked, pouring herself some juice.

"At a job site. Then he has to clean up some paperwork at his office. In fact, that's what I want to talk to you about." Lynda stacked the coupons to one side. "Have you thought about what you're going to do this summer?"

"I told Mom I want to get a job." Carrie sipped her orange juice.

"How would you feel about working in your dad's office? You can start Monday after school."

"Doing what?"

"Summer is his busiest time of the year. He's got more work than he can handle, and he's never caught up on his paperwork. Do you know he hasn't even sent out his snow-removal bills from last winter?"

"You're kidding!"

"I've finally talked him into hiring a full-time secretary, but she's swamped and needs help with typing and filing—stuff like that. With you helping—even part-time—by the end of the summer, she can have that office in some semblance of order."

Carrie turned the suggestion over in her mind. "I'm not sure. It would be hard for me to get there every day."

Lynda cleared her throat and leaned forward across the table. "Well, I had an idea about that also. Your dad misses you very much, Carrie."

"I miss him too, but I see him whenever I can."

"You could see him more if you lived with us this summer."

For a moment Carrie studied her juice glass. "I live with my mother," she said quietly.

"It would be just for the summer. Bobby misses you too. This is your home, and—"

"My mother needs me," Carrie interrupted. "She's busy with her job, but she'd hate living alone in our old house. I start dinner most nights when she's running late. She always tells me how nice it is to have me waiting when she comes in."

"Please don't be upset. It was just an idea. Your dad and I worry about you, that's all."

Carrie started to get angry. "Everybody treats me like a baby. I can take care of myself, you know."

"What if," Lynda paused, then said more firmly, "what if you got sick again?"

"But I won't. That's all behind me, and except for going for bloodwork, I hardly remember that I ever had leukemia."

"I'm sure Keith thought he was over it too."

"What do you know?" Carrie snapped. "Or Daddy either. He was so busy warring with Mom that I could have checked into a clinic in another state and never have been missed!"

"That's not true."

"*You* weren't even there!"

"I don't know about having cancer, Carrie, but I do know about being the kid of divorced parents."

Her frankness stopped Carrie cold. "Your parents were divorced?"

"When I was twelve. At least your parents have worked something out with you kids. At least your parents speak to one another. There was such hostility between my parents that my mother had to get a restraining order from the police. We couldn't even see Dad unless under court-approved supervision."

"I—I didn't know."

"It's over now, but I know how I felt at the time. I loved them both. I often wished there were two of me so I could stay with both of them." Lynda sighed and added, "That's why I put off getting married for so long. I'd promised myself that I'd never get divorced, and that if I ever had a family, I'd stay at home with them."

Carrie felt deflated; the fight had left her. "Then you know why I can't leave Mom. Dad has you and Bobby, Mom has me."

"But what about *you?*"

Carrie couldn't answer Lynda's question, so she ignored it. "As to working in Dad's office, I'd like to, but I don't see how I can manage it."

"I'll pick you up," Lynda said quickly and emphatically. "We'll create a work schedule for you, and I'll pick you up and take you home."

"That's an awful lot of driving." Carrie was mystified at Lynda's offer. It seemed like so much trouble for her to go to. "You'd do that for me?"

"Yes," Lynda said, her mouth set in a determined line. "For you, Carrie, and for your father too."

Carrie nodded. "All right. I'll work in Dad's office. Who knows? It might be fun." She offered Lynda a tentative smile as a sort of peace offering. She liked her stepmother and didn't want to be at odds with her. Besides, if Lynda came from a divorced family, she understood what Carrie was feeling, and that was more than anybody else in her life understood. Even Keith.

Chapter Ten

"Any news about your friend yet?" Lynda asked as she wound her way through the Monday-afternoon traffic.

"Not yet," Carrie said. "I'm going up to see him just as soon as I get off work today." At least Lynda had the courtesy to ask about Keith. Her mother was so wrapped up in her job and Larry Farrell that she barely acknowledged Carrie, much less Keith. And her father was pretty much ignoring him too.

"How will you get there?"

"The bus. And I don't care what Dad says. I'm gonna go see Keith, and that's that."

"You know I'd take you, but Bobby has a dentist appointment."

Carrie felt ashamed for snapping at Lynda. It wasn't her fault that no one in her family gave a darn about her friend.

"What's that?" Lynda asked, eyeing the glass bowl Carrie was carefully balancing on her lap.

"A terrarium. Keith's sort of an outdoor freak, so I got this fish tank and made a terrarium for him while he's in the hospital. Maybe he can look at it and feel a little like he's outside."

"That's thoughtful of you. I'm sure he'll like it."

Lynda's comments made Carrie feel better. Why was her stepmother the only one in her family who seemed to care? "I put in plants that grow without much attention. I guess that's what's nice about it—terrariums take care of themselves."

They arrived at the office, where her father's secretary put her right to work. Lynda had been right about one thing—her father was a very disorganized person. At five o'clock he walked in the door, grimy from the construction site. She couldn't hide her surprise and blurted, "Dad! Why are you here? Lynda said you'd be working till dark."

"She told me you're set on going to the hospital today. So I'm taking you."

She stared at him, bewildered. "Why?"

"So you don't have to ride the bus."

"But Daddy, Keith may be in the hospital for days. You can't take me all the time."

"Well, I can take you today for sure. I have to pick up some stuff for the job site, and the hospital's on the way."

"Thanks." She picked up the terrarium, and after climbing into his pickup, she said, "I'm capable of riding the bus, you know."

"I know. Lynda told me I was making too big a deal out of it. She says I have to stop thinking about you as a little girl, that you're fifteen. I have to learn to be more flexible."

Carrie was genuinely astounded. Not only had

Lynda gone to bat for her, but her father had listened. "Well, she's right."

"Are you two ganging up on me?"

"I hadn't thought about it until now, but it sounds like a good idea to me."

He groaned. "What'd I do to deserve this?"

Carrie started to talk to him then, to share her day and her impressions of his secretary and his unorganized office, and it seemed like only minutes later that the truck was pulling into the hospital parking lot. He didn't shut off the engine. "You could come up and see Keith," she said. "You said you liked him."

Her father shook his head. "No, I'm too dirty. The nurses would throw me out."

She watched his eyes shift away from the building, knowing it was more than that. What had she expected? He'd had a tough enough time visiting her, his own daughter, when she'd been sick. How could she expect him to visit a guy he hardly knew? Yet his heartlessness toward Keith irked her. Especially when she'd seen firsthand how open and caring Keith's family was toward each other.

Suddenly she saw her father's changed attitude in a whole new light. Maybe it was because he felt guilty about all the times he'd never visited her! They had talked about guilt in group meeting once—guilt sometimes made people act in a totally different way, going against their usual behavior. That was it, Carrie thought, feeling annoyed. Her father was feeling guilty, and now he was trying to make it up to her by taking her to the hospital and trying "to be more flexible."

"When he's out, ask him to come over for dinner or something."

"Sure," Carrie said, juggling the terrarium and shutting the truck's door a little too hard. "Thanks for the ride." She marched into the hospital without a backward glance, feeling entirely justified in being angry at her father. She didn't want him to try to make it up to her. It was too late. She'd hurt too much, been through too much to forgive either him or her mother for being unable to handle her leukemia. She'd had to handle it alone. And worse—she might have to handle it alone again.

Carrie was so busy stewing inwardly that she almost collided with Hella in the lobby. "Whoops!" Carrie said, with a smile that died on her lips. Hella looked troubled, and she could hardly even look Carrie in the eye. "What's wrong?" Carrie asked.

"It's been a long day," Hella said, but Carrie could sense that she was hedging.

Her pulse started thumping, and her stomach knotted. "No, it's something else." Hella said nothing. "It's Keith, isn't it?"

Hella shook her head. "You know I can't discuss a case with you."

"He's not just a 'case.' He's my friend."

Hella's expression looked torn and anguished. "Please, Carrie, don't put me on the spot."

She balanced the glass fish tank and announced, "I'm going upstairs."

Hella touched her shoulder. "Don't bother. Dr. Fineman's not letting anyone in his room."

"He'd want to see me."

"Maybe tomorrow."

Carrie felt cold all over. "I have to know what's going on."

"Let me take you home. Maybe you can call his family later. They've been here all day—his father's with him now—but I know Mrs. Gardner was taking the kids home."

Carrie rode back to her dad's with Hella, not speaking, trying to keep her mind from thinking too much. At home she put the terrarium in her room and then called Keith's, and when Mrs. Gardner answered, she begged to come over. Mrs. Gardner hesitated but finally said, "Yes, dear. Come over. Holly needs to see you."

Carrie paced the porch, and the minute Lynda turned into the driveway, she ran across the lawn, asking to be taken to Keith's house. She was grateful that Lynda didn't ask many questions, and fortunately Bobby was subdued after his visit to the dentist.

Purple shades of twilight were erasing the humid traces of day as she went to Keith's front door and rang the bell. The house looked dark and forlorn, though flowers bloomed in large cement pots on either side of the brick porch.

Mrs. Gardner opened the door, and Carrie waved to Lynda before stepping inside. "We're in the family room," she said, leading the way.

Holly and the others were either on the sofa or

stretched out on the floor. Carrie knew instantly that all of them had been crying. When Holly saw her, she leapt up and threw herself in Carrie's arms, sobbing. "You're here! Oh, I'm so glad you're here!"

Carrie began to cry too. Mrs. Gardner stroked both their heads. "Holly, dear. Poor Carrie doesn't even know what's going on. Let me talk to her." She gently peeled her daughter away, led Carrie to an overstuffed chair, and settled next to her on the armrest. She took Carrie's hand, and Carrie could see that her eyes were red and puffy. "We got the results of Keith's tests today."

It didn't take a genius to realize that the news was going to be bad. "And?" Carrie asked, her heart pounding.

"There's a tumor in his colon, and it's metastasized."

Carrie's gaze flew to Mrs. Gardner's face, and she felt the blood drain from her own. Keith's cancer had spread, and other tumors had grown. "Where?"

"His liver. I think Dr. Fineman suspected it when he examined Keith in the ER, but the tests confirmed it."

"What are they going to do about it? Can't they operate?"

"They can't simply remove a person's liver. You can't live without one."

"But there's got to be some drug! Some chemo or something!"

Mrs. Gardner put her hand over her eyes and took a long, shuddering breath. "There's nothing."

Carrie felt as if she were choking, as if she'd been underwater too long and couldn't reach the surface. "But that means—they can't give up! You can't let them."

Mrs. Gardner took her hand again, squeezing it so hard that Carrie's fingers went numb. "Dr. Fineman went over every option with us. The fact is, there are no options."

For Carrie time seemed to freeze, making that moment incredibly intense. The coolness of the darkened room, the floral scent of Mrs. Gardner's perfume, the quiet weeping of Holly and the others, burned everlasting impressions into her brain. She felt connected to these people, as if she'd become part of the family. "How long?"

"Dr. Fineman says making estimates isn't really fair. It's not a horse race."

"He has an idea. I know he does."

Mrs. Gardner sagged. "Maybe three months."

Fresh tears clogged her throat. "Only this summer?"

"Only this summer," Keith's mother echoed.

"I want to see him."

"In a couple of days. For now he says he just wants to be alone."

"But what can I do? There's got to be something I can *do*." Carrie stood and flapped her arms like a helpless bird.

"There's nothing any of us can do for him right now but pray. My son is dying . . . he's dying." She buried her face in her hands. Holly threw her arms around her mother. Gwen and April rushed over and embraced her too, while Jake hugged her lap and buried his teary face in her skirt.

Carrie stood back for only a moment; then she also reached around the circle, holding tightly to all of them. She pressed her trembling body against the huddle and filled her arms with the warm, soft substance of gathered grief.

Chapter Eleven

When Carrie walked into the support-group meeting, she felt as if every eye in the room had turned her way. She adjusted her sunglasses, feeling stupid for wearing them at night, but grateful to be able to hide behind them. Her eyes were so red and swollen from crying, she looked sickly herself.

Hella rushed over to her, saying, "Carrie, I'm so sorry. I'm sorry about Keith. I'm sorry I couldn't say anything to you in the lobby."

"It's all right. I know you couldn't. Besides, it was better hearing it from Keith's mom."

"Have you talked to him yet?" Carrie shook her head, unable to trust her voice. "He won't see anybody but his family," Hella said. "Mostly he just lies in bed and stares at the wall."

"That's what Holly tells me," Carrie managed, fumbling for a tissue. "I want to see him so bad."

"He'll come around. Give him some time."

Carrie glanced about the room. It was fuller than usual and much more subdued. She also realized that there were several more staff and clinic personnel than normal. "What's with all the suits?" she asked, sniffing.

"Support people. Every kid in the group is going to be impacted by this, even if they didn't know Keith well. We want to be here for those who need to hash out feelings about it."

"How do you think we feel?" Carrie snapped. "We feel lousy. It stinks. Keith's only sixteen years old." By now her voice and hands were shaking. A hush fell on people standing nearby, and Carrie felt embarrassed for raising her voice.

"It's all right to yell," Hella told her. "If you want, you can even throw something."

"I don't want to just throw something. I want to throw something *at* something."

"Like what?"

"Like all you medical types. Why can't you do anything for Keith? Why do we have to go through all the chemo and operations"—she gestured toward a boy on crutches with only one leg—"and the radiation, and all the tests and junk and then die! Why is that?"

Hella uttered a weary sigh. "Nothing's more frustrating than the practice of medicine, Carrie. And especially oncology. Cancer's not just one disease, it's a complicated bunch of diseases. For years cancer was an automatic death sentence, but today almost sixty percent of kids with leukemia survive."

"Is that supposed to make me feel better?"

Hella smiled wanly. "I suppose not. But it does make me feel better. It makes me feel like we're making some sort of headway against it."

"It makes me feel like I'm holding a lottery ticket,

and as someone calls out the winning combination, I look and see that my ticket is matching every number called. That's what happened to Keith, you know. All the numbers matched, except the very last one. 'So sorry, you lose, Keith,'" Carrie said in a sharp voice. She felt angry, but not at Hella, and she told her so.

"I know," Hella said. "That's what support group is all about. That's why we're here—so you can yell at us."

Carrie felt all mixed up inside. Keith had been handed the death sentence, but she kept seeing herself in his place, and that scared her most of all. She wasn't brave or heroic. She was plain and ordinary and incapable of handling such news for herself. And her parents weren't helping her much either.

When she'd told her father, he'd looked sick to his stomach and said, "You sure you want to hang around this boy? I don't want you getting all depressed."

"Of course, I want to hang around him!" she'd shouted back. "What kind of a friend do you think I am?"

It was Lynda who'd put her arm around Carrie's shoulder and said, "Stan, this isn't the time to ask such a thing."

But it had been her mom's reaction that had really shocked Carrie the most. She'd burst into tears! Why she'd hardly known Keith and had all but ignored Carrie when she'd talked of him. So Carrie had watched her weep, not sure of what to say. How could her mother get so affected by Keith's situation and yet act as if the same thing couldn't happen to her own daughter?

"Do you want me to give Keith a message from you?" Hella was asking.

Carrie pulled her thoughts away from her parents and nodded vigorously. "Please tell him that I have to see him, that he owes it to me. Tell him that I need my guitar lesson. That he made a deal—a promise—and I won't let him out of it."

"Guitar lesson?"

"He'll understand," she told Hella. "He *has* to."

Two days later Carrie stood outside Keith's hospital room, torn between crossing the threshold and turning around and leaving. Her arms ached from having carried the terrarium across the lobby, up on the elevator, and down the long corridor. Finally she stepped into the room, mostly because her hands were sweating and she was about to drop the glass tank.

Keith was sitting in a chair, and he was wearing street clothes. He waved casually, as if it had been only an hour since he'd last seen her instead of four days. She heaved the terrarium onto a nearby table and smiled. "You're dressed," she said, then felt stupid about stating the obvious.

"I'm going home," he said. "My dad's already checked me out, and my car's down in the parking lot. I thought I'd take you with me. Mom's baking a ham."

"Home?" She didn't know what she'd expected, but it hadn't been this.

"Yes. There's nothing else they can do for me, remember?" A sudden rush of tears filled her eyes. She bit her lip, hoping the pain would stop the flow. Keith came over and put his hands on her shoulders. "Can you halt the waterworks, Carrie? I don't think I can stand one more crying female. My sisters have been puddling up the place for days."

She nodded, unable to speak. He dropped his hands and studied the terrarium. "So what's this?"

She cleared her throat. "I—uh—made it for you because I know how you like the great outdoors. But I guess you won't be needing it. You can go outside now."

"It's neat," he said, peering through the glass at every angle. "Thanks. Dad took my other stuff, so let's take it down to the car. I want to get out of this place."

They left without saying good-bye at the nurses' station, and once outside Keith paused, turned his face skyward, and drew in a deep breath. "Boy, I've missed being outside." She watched him and wondered how much longer he had to feel the sun on his face. During the ride to his house, he kept the radio turned up loud, so they didn't talk much. And at his house his family swarmed over him, hugging and touching and telling him how glad they were he was finally home.

Later they ate baked ham and mashed potatoes and green beans—all of Keith's favorites. Carrie kept feeling as if she'd fallen into a time warp and the past few days hadn't happened and Keith was perfectly fine. Jake's cheerful patter brought reality sharply into focus, however, when he asked, "After you're dead, will you come back for my birthday party?"

For a moment no one spoke. Carrie wondered how they would explain the finality of death to a five-year-old. Mr. Gardner said, "Dead people don't come back to see us, Jake. We go see them in heaven when we die."

Jake scrunched up his forehead. "Not even for birthdays and Christmas?"

"Not even then."

"Boy, it's gonna be a crummy Christmas if Keith's not here," the child said.

Carrie watched Keith wipe his palms along his jeans. He said, "Let's get that guitar lesson going, Carrie."

"Oh, but you don't have to—"

"Come on," he said, pushing back from the table and heading to his room.

Carrie glanced around the table at his family's stricken faces. "Go on," Mrs. Gardner said. "Do what he wants to do."

Carrie found him in his room, sitting on his bed Indian style, plucking at the strings of his guitar. The notes quivered with a vibrato that made a lump stick in her throat. She sat across from him on the bed. "I'll understand if you want to back out of our deal. Helping you cram for exams is sort of dumb now, I guess. Besides, exams are next week already, so you probably won't be taking them."

"When they told me that the cancer was in my liver, I didn't believe it," Keith said, shrugging off her comments about exams. "I figured, 'Man, what a bummer! Now what? What kind of torture's in store for me to cure this complication?'" He gave her a sad smile. "Surprise. No treatment."

"Hella told me the same thing at support group. The doctors act like they know so much, but they really don't." Carrie found herself torn over wanting to talk about Keith's diagnosis with him.

"How's everybody takin' it in the group?"

"Pretty hard."

"You gotta promise me something."

"Anything."

"After I'm—you know—gone, I want you to have a big party with the whole group. I don't want everybody standing around and crying and acting all sad. You throw the biggest, best party ever. Will you?"

She nodded. "Will you come to any more meetings?"

"I don't think so. No use bringing people down."

"What will you do?" She asked the question haltingly.

"I spent days thinking about it. I talked to my dad too. We decided no one was going to stand around whispering about me dying. No secrets—it was all gonna be out in the open. That's why Jake asked the question he did tonight. No use trying to protect him from the truth."

"Aren't you scared?"

His green eyes bore into hers. "Yeah, I'm scared. I don't want to die, Carrie." His voice faltered, and she thought she'd burst into tears. "But God didn't consult me, and I didn't get a vote. I talked to Dr. Fineman about what to expect. He's seen lots of people die.

"He was honest with me. He told me I'd be all right for a while, but when I started going down, I could come to the hospital, and they would hook me up to IVs and respirators and monitors. That way I could live a little longer and not be in pain."

She shivered but asked, "When do you go back?"

"I'm not." His eyes were clear and bright. "I'm never going back to the hospital again."

Chapter Twelve

Carrie blinked, as if she hadn't heard him correctly. He toyed with the guitar. "Have you ever heard of hospice?"

"I've heard the word, but I don't know what it is."

"I talked with Hella about it. She works with the program through the hospital. It's a way of letting cancer patients die at home with their families to support them and without hurting. Nurses and social workers and all those types help the patients and then their families after the person dies. Hospice lets you die in your own home, in your own bed and not alone."

Carrie recoiled. "That sounds awful! Like people are just standing around waiting for you to croak."

He shook his head. "That's not it at all, but when doctors tell you, 'We can't do anything else for you,' you start thinking about what choices you've got left. The way I see it, you get one: you can decide *where*. I don't want it to be in a hospital with that stinking smell of medicine all around me."

"But you're safer in the hospital. There're nurses and doctors and machines. They can help you live longer."

"How long? A few more weeks? What difference

can a few lousy weeks make?" His voice rose, and she realized how upset he was about it. "And think about my family. Right now I just want to make it as easy on them as possible. I don't want them taking shifts around my hospital bed. No, that's not for me. This way hospice people will be with us all the way. None of us will have to be alone."

"But none of you are alone," she burst out. He had no idea what it was to be alone as she did.

"Wrong. We're alone all right. After the doctors know for sure that you're beyond their treatments and cures, they act like you don't exist. Oh, they were nice to me in the hospital—you know—polite after the prognosis came in. But once they knew there was nothing left to do medically, well—I became a non-person, an embarrassment to them. Business as usual went on around me, but it didn't concern me. It's hard to explain."

Somehow she understood. "So what will you do now?"

Keith laid the guitar down on the bed. "I'm going into the hospice program. That means no more treatments to stop the cancer."

"Nothing?" Her hands had gone cold.

"Just medicine for pain—all that I need to keep from hurting."

"But—but you could get addicted," she cried.

A bemused smile appeared. "Believe me, becoming a junkie is not a major worry to me."

She flushed, embarrassed. Of course it wouldn't be. "And your parents are gonna let you do this?"

"I told you once before that my folks have always encouraged us to make our own decisions."

"But this is different!"

"No it isn't. Nothing's going to change the fact that I'm dying. This way my family can be with me every step of the way—Mom and Dad, my sisters, and Jake."

She felt alone and cut off. He was being taken from her in every way. At least in the hospital she could slip in and stand by his bed, but this way— She abruptly asked, "So what happens next?"

"There're some things I want to do while I still feel good enough to do them and before I have to start taking megadoses of painkillers. I told my parents that I want all of us to go up to the cabin for a week."

Carrie knew how much he loved the woods, and part of her wanted him to be able to go. But part of her was bitterly disappointed. She wanted to be with him for as long as she could. "When are you going?"

"As soon as school's out."

Tears filled her throat, and she dropped her gaze. "I'm glad."

"Carrie," he said, his voice very quiet. "I want you to come too. Please."

"Me? You want me to come?"

"Don't panic," he said with a hint of a smile. "There's indoor plumbing and everything."

"I want to come, Keith. More than anything. It's just that I'm not sure if I can persuade my parents. They expect me to work."

"But you'll ask them?"

"Of course I'll ask." Already her mind was spinning, thinking of the best way to approach them. "Your family won't mind?" she asked.

"They want me to have whatever I want. Besides, who's gonna say no to a dying kid's wish?"

He'd made the remark in sardonic jest, but it made her stomach tighten. *A dying kid's wish*. "Not me," she told him.

He buried his face in his hands. "This isn't the way I planned for this summer to go." His voice sounded muffled. "I'm still sort of numb about the whole thing. It's like my brain is divided into two parts." He looked at her again. "One part says, 'This is just a bad dream. You'll wake up any minute now.' And the other part says, 'You gotta get ready, Keith. You gotta get things together because soon it's all gonna be over.'"

"What does 'over' really mean?" she asked, as much for her sake as his.

"I'm still working on it."

"If you figure it out, will you tell me?"

"You'll be the first."

She smiled. "Who's on first?"

"What," he answered.

"What's on second," she whispered.

"Three strikes and you're out," he said, abruptly changing the flow of the Abbott and Costello routine. "*I'm* out. What a lousy finish for my game."

Carrie asked her mother first about going to the Gardner's cabin. Faye stared at her, making eye con-

tact via the mirror on her dresser. "I can understand
your attraction to him, Carrie, but to stand around
watching him die—" She shuddered. "I can't imagine
doing such a thing."

I know, Mother, Carrie thought. Aloud she said,
"I'd still like to go."

"It must be hard on his mother," Faye added ab-
sently. "No one ever expects to bury her own child."

"Keith's family is pretty close. They want to all be
together for as long as possible."

Faye shrugged her shoulders in resignation. "If
you want to go, it's all right by me. Besides, it'll give
me an opportunity to start painting the inside of the
house."

"What?" Carrie asked, feeling as if she'd missed
an important line in a book. How could her mother
switch between Keith's dying to house painting?

"Larry said he'd help, so we're going to repaint.
You know, sort of spruce everything up. With you out
for a week, it'll go quicker. Do you want to pick the
color for your room?"

"Surprise me," she said. Carrie felt a million
miles apart from her mother just then, as if they'd
come from separate universes. And besides, what did
Larry have to do with anything? This wasn't his house.

"I'll probably go with a pale pink. That'll be nice
for a little girl's room."

Carrie started to tell her she wasn't a little girl
anymore, that having cancer and watching kids die
from cancer sort of took her out of the "little girl" cate-
gory. But her mother was spreading night cream

across her cheeks and throat and humming to herself in the mirror. Carrie said nothing, because she realized that her mother wouldn't have truly heard her anyway.

Getting her father's permission to go to the Gardeners' cabin wasn't so simple. "What about your job?" he asked.

"This is more important than any job," she said.

"I don't like the idea. It doesn't seem right, with him dying and all."

"Mom said it was okay with her."

"Where does she get off giving you permission without checking with me?"

What was the matter with her parents? This wasn't a contest to see who was the boss or to figure out who was calling the shots for her life. Neither was it a pajama party with some of her friends. It was important that she go. Couldn't they see that? This could happen to *her*, and then how would they act?

"You should be living here with me and Lynda and Bobby," her father said.

"I'm not walking out on Mom," she said defiantly.

His face turned red. "I didn't walk out on her."

"She needs me," she said stubbornly.

"She doesn't need anyone," her father told her, then clamped his lips together tightly.

This wasn't getting them anywhere. Carrie didn't want to antagonize him, so she said, "It'll just be for a week. You can spare me from the office for a week."

"I want time to think about it."

"But they want to leave as soon as school's out."

"I said I'll think about it."

In the end he'd agreed, but Carrie was certain that it had been Lynda's doing. At least she had one ally in this battle. Why couldn't her mother be more like Lynda? Perhaps if she had been, there would have been no divorce, no tug-of-war for Carrie's allegiance. But there was still her cancer. Could Lynda cope with *that*?

Chapter Thirteen

~~~

The Gardner's cabin sat at the upper end of a winding dirt road, on the crest of a Carolina mountain-top. The surrounding woods were lush and green, so thick that Carrie was reminded not of a forest, but of an ocean. The shades of green sparkled in every imaginable hue, broken only by the brown of tree bark and the white flowering of Queen Anne's lace.

It had taken nearly all day to drive there in the van, but Carrie thought the trip fun. Keith had slept most of the way in a makeshift bed in the back, while she and Holly and the others had played cards and word games across the seats. They ate lunch from a picnic basket Mrs. Gardner had prepared, snacked on chocolate-chip cookies and popcorn, and sang endless rounds of camp songs.

Carrie considered them a fantastic family. They had heated discussions, but there was always an atmosphere of caring and concern for others' feelings. Yet what impressed her most was the way Keith's parents responded and acted. They never yelled or argued and intervened only when a compromise between factions couldn't be worked out.

Throughout the trip Carrie saw Mrs. Gardner

reach over and stroke her husband's arm, or him squeeze her hand and smile. The gestures seemed very intimate, and at first she felt guilty about watching. Yet they never appeared ashamed about openly showing their affection. She wondered what it would have been like to have been raised by such people but decided that the wondering was too complicated— sort of like peering into a maze of mirrors and trying to discern which reflected object was the "real" one.

The scenery changed gradually as the van left behind the Ohio valley and climbed across the Cumberland Gap, winding its way into the Smoky Mountains. Her first glimpse of the cabin was late that afternoon. It was larger than she'd imagined, constructed of dark logs held in place with grout and pitch. Most of the structure looked weathered, but the new addition jutting off to one side looked fresh and unmarked by rain and sun.

Inside, a breakfast bar separated the kitchen area from the great room, and a large stone fireplace stretched along one wall. The air smelled stale, and everyone set about dispelling the musty odor by flinging open windows. In the room Carrie was to share with Keith's sisters, there were double bunk beds and white eyelet curtains that fluttered in the mountain breeze. Jake bounded from room to room, squealing with delight and babbling excitedly. Each one had a mission, a task to accomplish, except Carrie, so she wandered out onto a rustic back porch and studied the surrounding woods.

"Didn't I tell you it was beautiful up here?" Keith asked, coming up behind her.

"It's beautiful, all right. And the cabin's really nice. Maybe I should help your sisters make up the beds and unpack."

"They can do it. Come on, we'll go for a walk."

She didn't need any urging. She was anxious to explore the scenery, so she followed him down a trail, and moments later, when she turned, the cabin had been swallowed by the trees. "Can you find your way back?"

"I'm an ace explorer, remember?"

"Yes, but can you find your way back?"

He laughed. "Don't worry, I've spent every summer since I was seven in these woods. I want to show you the lake."

They walked downward, along a sloping path lined by variegated shrubs. The air was dry and cool and smelled of the sweet, untamed scent of wildflowers. "I didn't think it'd be so cool in June," she said.

"We're in the mountains, remember. At night you have to wear a sweater."

"I don't think I brought one."

"I'll loan you a sweatshirt."

In front of them the woods thinned out. Grass appeared, the ground grew softer, more spongy. The lake burst into full view, causing Carrie to catch her breath. They stood shoulder to shoulder at the water's edge and looked across its shining gray green expanse.

"It's the afternoon sunlight," Keith told her. "First thing in the morning, the color's a dark navy blue."

Speckles of sunshine danced over the surface, reminding Carrie of jeweled sequins. "It's so big," she said. "Is it deep?"

"Sure is." Abruptly he yanked off his shoes and socks and started to wade. "Come on," he told her.

She stepped into the water and felt soft mud squish between her toes. "It's like ice."

"There's an underground spring that feeds it from inside the mountain. When I was a kid, I used to imagine I could find the spring, go underwater, and swim through a hole into a prehistoric world underneath the lake."

"I used to imagine that a starship would come for me and take me away to another planet," she confessed shyly because she'd never told another person in the world about that fantasy. "Especially when they'd do bone-marrow aspirations. It helped, you know. Pretending that I was out in the stars instead of lying on that table with some lab person jabbing my bones and sucking them out. It hurt. It really hurt."

"I used to always pretend I was here at the lake when they'd do my lab work," he said. "Did you ever dream that you were a bird and could fly?"

"I sure have. And in the dream I could actually see things from a bird's-eye view—flying over roofs and treetops and mountains. In the dream it seems so real. How do you figure that we can see things so realistically when we've never even flown before?"

"I read once that some scientists think we might have some sort of collective memory."

"I thought you didn't read," she teased.

He kicked a spray of water her way, and she dodged. "These guys think that when we crawled out of the slime we kept some sort of primitive recollection of it. So as we evolved into birds, we kept the recollection of flight too."

Carrie wrinkled her nose. "Do you believe that?"

"Not for a minute."

They laughed, and the sound floated over the lapping water and into the trees. "So where did we come from?" she asked.

His green eyes danced. "Don't you know where you came from, Carrie? Didn't your mom ever tell you about the birds and the bees?"

"Very funny." She trudged out of the water and found a grassy spot and sat down. She rubbed her toes, which were numb from the chilly water. Keith's shadow fell across her, and she looked up. The sun was directly behind him, sending darts of light into the sky and making his body seem ethereal, otherworldly. For a moment her heart hammered, and she was filled with an unbearable aching.

He lowered himself beside her, plucked a blade of grass, and chewed on it. "For me, Carrie, where I came from doesn't matter. What matters right now is where I'm going."

His mood had changed. Pensiveness had replaced the teasing and joking. "Maybe you'll come back as a bird," she ventured.

"Reincarnated?" he asked. "That's not for me. Who wants to live again as an ant or a dog?" He raised himself up on his elbow and stared at her hard. "I want to be *me*. Always and forever—I want to be Keith Gardner."

"You'd make a cute puppy," she joked, because she wasn't prepared to think about the hereafter. Yet the thought nibbled at the back of her mind. "Forever seems like such a long time to be away from all of this," she mused, gesturing to the lake and trees. She realized that she never wanted to be anything other than Carrie Blake either. As hard as it was sometimes, she still wanted to be herself.

"Maybe it's sort of like falling asleep," Keith ventured. "Nothing hurts when you're sound asleep. Time passes, and you don't even know it."

"But sleepers wake up," she reminded him. "What about dead people? Maybe they don't ever wake up."

He balled his fist around a clump of grass, as if touching it anchored him to the earth. "I think about being put into a hole in the ground where it's very dark. I think about never seeing the sun again, or feeling the wind, or smelling flowers. My mind can't accept that, you know? It can't picture nothingness."

She shuddered, because she couldn't picture it either. "So we don't believe in reincarnation, and we don't believe in a forever of nothingness. What do we believe in?"

"I guess that's where God comes into things," he said simply. "God and heaven and all that stuff. I think about going to heaven when I die and meeting God one on one."

An egret lifted from the far side of the lake. It was white and slender, and its feathers reflected the sun. "Why do you suppose God made the world so beautiful, then won't let us live in it forever?"

"I'll ask him when I see him," Keith told her. He paused then continued, "Doctors bring people back from the 'dead' by restarting their hearts, but even when medical technology can save someone, that person will still die someday. We all have to die eventually."

"I know, but—"

Keith cut her off. "When Ma was carrying Jake, she let us put our hands on her stomach and feel the baby kick. That was so *weird*. I'd seen pictures in books, but I couldn't imagine a real live baby inside of her, all curled up in a ball with no room to move. I used to think how awful it must be to be all cramped up in the dark when it's so beautiful out here in the world. But then I realized that maybe for Jake it was okay to be that way because he didn't know anything else. I mean, how do you explain sunlight to someone who's never seen it? This life is great, but how do we know there's not something better after this life is over?"

His eloquent words reached inside Carrie and made her less afraid. She wanted to tell him, but just then they heard twigs snapping as someone came crashing through the trees. Carrie bolted to her feet and turned to face her foe, but it was Holly who burst through the foliage, not an avenging angel.

Holly stopped and stared from one to the other, her expression reminding Carrie of someone who'd stumbled onto a scene she wasn't prepared to see. She guessed she and Keith must look pretty serious, so she asked brightly, "Going for a swim?"

"No, I was looking for you two. Mom's got supper ready, and we couldn't find you, and we were worried, and . . ." Her voice trailed off.

"Daniel Boone here promised to show me the lake and not get lost. We started talking and lost track of time. Sorry."

Keith rose slowly, painfully, by Carrie's estimation. But his voice was light. "So they send out a hound dog to find us."

"A *dog*!" Holly cried. "You call me a dog? Prepare to die, fiend!" She ran toward him, feigning terrible retaliation but stopped short in front of him, realizing what she'd said.

Keith reached out and touched his sister's cheek. "That's why I came here to the cabin," he said tenderly. "That's why I came."

Chapter Fourteen

Keith's words stayed with Carrie for days. She understood now that his coming to the cabin was really more complex than seeing his favorite place one last time. For Keith it had become a ritual of leaving, of bidding farewell not simply to a place, but to the world, people, to time itself. In months, perhaps weeks, he would step into a realm where they could not follow. This week would somehow prepare him for that transition.

Sadly she felt it was not to be so simple for her. She felt torn in half—some moments prepared to relinquish her medical status of remission so that she could go with him, and other times adamant about staying in the bright green world until she withered from old age. Still, in spite of the seriousness, the time she spent with Keith's family was also idyllic.

She caught tadpoles at the edge of the lake with Jake and the girls in the early morning. She lay in the noonday sun beside Holly and went hiking along twisting trails where she picked buckets of wild blackberries that Mrs. Gardner turned into succulent pies. After hiking she'd come back ravenous and sit down to enormous meals and cleanup periods marked by dishtowel wars and soap-bubble contests. In the evenings they all played Monopoly at the round oak dining table.

Keith slept frequently. Carrie knew that he took more pain pills as the week progressed, but whenever he felt able, he'd join them for cards and board games. Some evenings he simply stayed on the sofa, watching them play. Carrie often felt his gaze before she saw his eyes on her. It was as if they were linked by some strange telepathic power—mentally joined like surgically separated Siamese twins. They spoke without speaking, communicated without language.

He spent one long afternoon fishing with his father in a boat on the lake while Carrie and the others swam. After swimming she lay on a towel next to Holly and let the noonday sun remove the chill of the water from her skin. Jake came over with his bottle of tadpoles.

"Look!" he cried. "See, they got legs." Carrie and Holly squinted through the glass. Sure enough, the wiggling tads had lost their tails and grown webbed appendages.

"That's cool," Holly said. "You know, pretty soon you'll have to put them back in the lake."

"Why? I wanna take 'em home. They can keep live in the bowl with my goldfish."

"They're amphibians and just start out in the water. Then they breathe air like you and me, so they need dry land."

"No way, they can just keep swimming."

"She's right, sport," Carrie said. "I took biology

this year, and frogs need water *and* land. My teacher said so."

"Aw, you're making that up."

"Go ask Mom."

Jake grabbed up his bottle. "I will," he said, marching off.

Carrie giggled. "I think you ruined his dream of frog farming."

"Just what we need—a frog dynasty." Holly rolled her eyes. She stretched out on her stomach, propped up on her elbows, chin in hand. "I'm glad you came on this trip," she told Carrie.

"I am too." Carrie shut her eyes against the overhead glare of the sun.

"Do you like my brother?" Holly blurted the question.

"Of course."

"No, I mean do you *really* like my brother—like a boyfriend?"

Carrie turned her head and saw the pensive expression on Holly's face. Carefully she turned on her side. Emotions churned inside her as she remembered the times she'd sneaked longing looks at Keith during support-group meetings, or felt her tummy flutter when he passed her in the halls at school. And then when they'd actually gotten together, their illness had become their common bond.

But something had changed over the months. She liked him, but with more than gooey feelings and sweaty palms. She cared about him, longed to be with him, wanted to talk to him, tell him her deepest secrets and favorite dreams.

Carrie said, "I've never had a boyfriend before. Some of my friends have them, but when they were going crazy over some guy in their class, I was on chemo and I was bald and ugly and worried about keeping my lunch down."

She thought, *And my parents were splitting up, and I felt like a yo-yo between them,* but how could Holly understand that part? She said, "I guess I never had time to think about having a boyfriend."

"But you're pretty now. I wish I looked like you."

Her words surprised Carrie. To her, Holly was cute and bubbly, open and friendly. She told her so, but the younger girl shrugged away the compliment. "I'm skinny and flat-chested and better at sports than most guys—which is a turnoff for most of them. I'm scared to death of starting at Martin High next year."

Holly plucked at the nap on her towel. "I always thought Keith would be there for me. I had this idea that he'd have a girlfriend, and I'd meet a neat guy, and we'd all double-date and have so much fun."

Carrie saw the image all too clearly as Holly talked. It was simple to see herself as Keith's girlfriend. "But it can't be," Carrie said miserably.

"Oh, I'm not so sure," Holly said in a mysterious tone.

Carrie studied the girl's profile, the wide brown eyes and straight nose, so much like Keith's. "What do you mean?"

"I think Keith's gonna get well."

"Oh, Holly, I don't know—"

Holly rolled on her side to face Carrie. Her eyes, dark and serious, held a conspiratorial gleam. "I've been praying every day. I promised God that if he cured Keith, I'd become a nun."

"But you're not even Catholic."

"It doesn't matter. I've promised him that I'll never get married and live my whole life in India helping the poor like Mother Theresa."

Carrie recalled making pacts with God to keep her parents from getting divorced, but her offers had fallen on deaf ears. She wanted to tell Holly that her vows were useless—God did whatever he felt like. "Have you—uh—told Keith what you're doing?"

"Oh no," Holly confessed. "I want the miracle to happen, and then I'll tell him why it happened. I think if I tell him before, it might get jinxed or something. The doctors can't cure him," Holly continued. "A miracle's his only hope."

"And you'd do that? Become a nun in India if it would give Keith a miracle?"

"Of course! He's my brother," Holly said, flattening onto her tummy position. "I mean, boys are mostly idiots—except for Keith of course. Who wants to get married anyway?" She rested her chin on upturned palms. "Still, I might date a little. You don't think that would spoil the deal if I dated, do you?"

Carrie felt like crying but couldn't explain why. "It's hard to say," she said evasively.

The sun had evaporated the water on her skin by

now, and she rose and stared out to where Keith and his father were fishing on the lake.

She watched as Mr. Gardner cast his fly rod outward. She could just make out Keith, who was reclining in the stern. She knew instinctively how he was feeling physically. He'd be slightly nauseous; exposure to the sun did that sometimes. He'd be weak too, and sort of drifting in a stupor of pain medication.

If only Holly's pact would work. If only Keith could get well. She glanced down at Holly's resting body and wondered if never getting married for the sake of her brother's cure wasn't such a bad trade-off. At least she'd never have to endure divorce and making kids choose which parent to live with. Holly would always have a home, always have a place that was her very own if she was doing something worthwhile like serving mankind.

But she thought about what Keith had said. No matter if a miracle saved him or not, he'd eventually wind up right back in the same place. Carrie sighed and announced, "I'm going in the water." She ran and dived, welcoming the wet, biting chill as it closed over her. Under the surface the world was dark and primordial. She curled up into a ball and wished she'd never have to come up for air. But of course that was impossible. She'd already seen the sun.

That night Keith made her perform solo on the guitar for his family. "I'm not ready," she sputtered.

"Sure you are. You know all the chords, and

you've been practicing every day. It's time to knock 'em dead."

"When they hear me play, they'll die all right," she grumbled. Yet in spite of her nervousness, she sat cross-legged in front of the fireplace and strummed the instrument.

Keith sat on the sofa, and Jake and the girls scooted around her in a semicircle. Mr. and Mrs. Gardner pulled chairs from the oak table behind the others. Carrie's mouth went dry. It shouldn't be such a big deal, she told herself. She looked at Keith, who gave her a thumbs-up signal, then she lowered her head over the neck of the guitar and played.

The tune wasn't masterfully performed, but as the last notes faded, Carrie smiled at her small audience. They applauded. "Excellent!" Holly cried.

Carrie blushed, but she felt good. She looked at Keith, whose expression said, "I told you so."

"Encore!" Mr. Gardner shouted.

"Sorry, that's the only tune I know," Carrie told him. They clapped again, and she quipped, "Is that 'cause it's over?"

April tossed a sofa pillow at her, and then Holly jumped her, followed by the others. They rolled and tumbled on the floor, tickling each other and laughing until Carrie's sides hurt and she couldn't catch her breath. She finally cried for mercy, and while she smoothed her hair and retucked her T-shirt, she looked once more toward Keith.

His face was etched with a lonely, melancholy look that made her smile fade and turned her insides cold. There would have been a time when he would have been rolling on the floor with them, a time when he would have led the tickle session.

"I need to lie down," he said.

"Are you okay?" his mother asked.

"Just tired," he said. But when he rose, Carrie noticed that he held his side and that he shuffled when he walked. She wanted to cry, but of course she couldn't. She wanted to scream, but she couldn't do that either. She watched him disappear into his bedroom, and as the door shut, she saw it as a symbol of closing them all out from a world he had to explore, where she could not follow.

Chapter Fifteen

~

Carrie awoke with a start. The bedroom was quiet, draped in shadow. From below her came the rhythmic sounds of Holly's breathing, and in the next bunk April and Gwen slept peacefully too. She wasn't sure what had awakened her, but something had.

Moonlight shimmered through the lacy curtain, casting leafy patterns from the trees. She was drawn to the window by the eerie beauty of the light. Quietly she climbed down from the upper bunk and pulled aside the curtain. Overhead the moon glowed like a translucent pearl. She pressed her palm against the pane of glass and felt the cold mountain air seep through.

She heard a gentle rapping on the bedroom door and padded quickly across the room and opened it. Keith stood there, fully dressed. She shielded her nightshirt-clad body from him with the door. "What are you doing up?" she asked. Her heart pounded, suddenly afraid for him. "Are you all right?"

"I can't sleep. I want to go down to the lake. Will you come?"

She glanced nervously back toward the sleeping girls. "Right now? Yeah, I—I guess so."

"It's cold," he said, and passed a hooded sweat-shirt through the open crack. "I'll be waiting out on the porch."

She dressed hurriedly, pulling on the sweatshirt, even though it was much too large. It carried the scent of him—talc mingled with cherry Lifesavers. She met him on the porch and followed him down the now-familiar path to the lake. Sounds of katydids, frogs, and night insects sang through the woods. The moon lit up the world.

At the edge of the water, he stopped, and she came up beside him, remembering the first time they'd stood there together. Now the lake looked black except for a glimmering silver path paved by the moon.

"We'll be leaving tomorrow," he said. "I couldn't waste my last night here sleeping. I hope you don't mind."

"I don't mind." She knew that today had been their last full day but couldn't face going. "I wish we had a time garden," she said wistfully. "I read about one in a science-fiction story once. It was full of special flowers that had the ability to hold back time. Whenever you were in the garden, time couldn't touch you. Nothing ever got old. Nothing ever died."

"I wish I'd read more," Keith said. "Funny how you think about all the things you wish you had done when you don't have the time to do them ever again."

From far across the lake, a whippoorwill called to its mate. "I guess everybody thinks he's got plenty of

• time to do things," she said. "That's the way it should be, you know. It's not fair to rob people of time."

"You're not gonna get all teary on me are you?"

"Never," she lied, swiping her hand across her eyes. She turned to him and peered up to his face, which was washed by the moon's light. "Holly thinks you're going to be cured by a miracle."

Keith shrugged his shoulders. "I guess miracles can happen. But I don't think one's going to happen to me. You tell her that. In fact, Carrie, I'm feeling worse every day, and I'm taking more pain pills. My legs and feet are holding fluid too. The swelling is making my clothes feel tight."

She understood what he was saying, and it frightened her. Time was running out. But it also made her angry because he wasn't hoping for a miracle. She wanted him to believe enough to make one happen. "I don't see anything wrong in hoping for a miracle," she said, hugging her shoulders tightly. "You don't have to be so resigned to dying, you know."

"Listen, we've been through this already. I know what's happening to me, and I'm ready for it."

"Well, I'm not."

"I know where I'm going, and I'm ready for that too."

"Heaven?" she asked.

"If God'll let me in," he answered.

"Well, since you're going first, will you look out for me when I come along?" She hadn't meant to ask such a thing, had never meant to blurt out her deepest, innermost fears, but he seemed at peace about it all, and she had peace about nothing.

Keith cocked his head, and his gaze was so intense that she almost turned and walked away. "You can't ever think this will happen to you," he said slowly.

"Cancer's terminal," she told him, trembling as she spoke.

"*Life's* terminal," he said. "You've never had a relapse, never had a problem."

"Neither had you," she countered.

"You can't measure yours by mine. Where's that 'never give up' attitude you're so famous for?"

"Maybe I'm just tired of the whole mess. Maybe I'm sick and tired of watching my friends suffer. It's like we hurt and hurt, and there's no way out of it. The doctors can't help us. Mommies can't kiss us and make us well. God won't do a miracle. What's left?"

He laced his fingers through hers. "Just because this is happening to me now, there's no reason for you to think it's going to be the same way for you. We all aren't asked to die when we're sixteen."

"But you *did* have plans," she sniffed, afraid to look him in the eye. "You wanted to play baseball."

"You wanted to be on the Carson show. You can still do that."

"How can I? You were supposed to follow me on the guitar, remember? Now you're leaving me all alone." The words tasted bitter.

"For me . . . it's over. But not for you."

"How is it different for me? What can I do?"

He studied her in the moonlight, brushed her hair away from her cheek, and rested his hand on the nape of her neck. "You can *live*. For all of us who can't, Carrie. You *can*."

"But I don't want you to die. I'll miss you so much. We all will . . . the people who care about you." She caught herself because she was just about to say "love you," and she didn't love him. She didn't. Love was supposed to make a person feel good, and now she only hurt—hurt so bad. "How can we go on without you?" She began to cry and hated herself for breaking down in front of him.

Moonlight splashed his face, and he looked agonized. She threw her arms around him. He held her too, and his embrace was so tight she could scarcely breathe. She hugged him all the harder, as if by doing so she could absorb him into her skin and somehow hold onto him forever. They stood in the moonlight, with the sounds of the lake all around them and the scent of night-blooming jasmine heavy in the summer air until Carrie stopped crying. They pulled apart, and Carrie felt chilled, slightly embarrassed. Furiously she wiped the sleeve of the sweatshirt over her face. "I— I'm sorry," she mumbled. "I know you don't like crying girls."

He'd retreated to the edge of the clearing and was picking bark off a tree. "I felt like crying too," he confessed. He pulled a pocket knife from his jeans and started carving at the trunk. Slowly she saw his and her initials emerge. Beneath them he etched: *Keith was here*.

"You come back someday, Carrie, and you look for this, all right? You find my name and tell people that I really existed, that I was a real, *live* person."

She touched the freshly carved scars and felt as if they were chiseled across her heart. "No one could ever forget you," she said.

"You'll keep in touch with my family?"

"You know I will."

"You'll sort of watch out for Holly next year at Martin?"

"I promise."

He closed the knife, crooked his arm around her shoulders, and together they slid to the ground, Keith pressing his back to the tree trunk. She leaned against his chest, held her ear to his heart, and listened to it beat. The rumble of bullfrogs seemed to play in harmony. Overhead the moon dipped lower, and the stars began to go out as dawn approached in the east.

She willed the sun away, hoping to hold onto the night, the stars, the slice of time that held them. But they were not in a time garden. And she could not stop the rising of the sun. Hoping he wouldn't notice, Carrie wept again, the tears, soft and silent, ran down her cheeks and dampened the front of his jacket. And this time he did not ask her to stop.

After breakfast they all worked together to close up the house and pack the van. There was little discussion, little horseplay, and they worked quickly. Mr. Gardner stacked pillows along the back bench seat, and Keith lay down. Carrie kept eyeing him anxiously. His skin had taken on a yellowish tinge, and his face looked puffy.

They drove back toward Ohio silently; even Jake ceased his chatter. He sat clutching his jar of half-formed frogs, his legs dangling over the edge of the seat, his head of tangled hair catching the sun. The image caused a lump in Carrie's throat that she couldn't explain.

It was twilight when they rounded the familiar street of her neighborhood. She stared out the window as they passed along the long row of two-story houses. A sprinkler spun and splattered the side of the van, and the next-door neighbor's dog barked as they pulled into the driveway.

She saw her home looming in the half light, lamps aglow from living-room windows. At least her mother hadn't forgotten that she was coming home, she thought, relieved. From the corner of her eye, she saw a small rectangular square rising on the lawn. In the semidarkness she could just make out the bold lettering. It read: For Sale.

Chapter Sixteen

~~~

"But you can't sell our house, Mom! You just can't." Carrie stood in the middle of the kitchen, her suitcase and duffel bags surrounding her feet where she dropped them after rushing in the door.

"Good gracious, Carrie. Stop making such a fuss. You haven't even noticed how nicely Larry and I fixed it up."

"But why fix it up if you're going to sell it?"

"*That's* why I fixed it up," her mother told her, pouring herself a cup of tea from the kettle that whistled angrily on the stove.

"But all you said was that you were going to do some repainting. You were just going to paint my room—"

"Oh, and it's such a perfect shade of pink. You'll love it."

"Why should I love it if I'm moving?"

"Sit down and stop yelling." Faye demanded. "Let me explain."

Carrie jerked a chair away from the table, causing a screeching sound. She plopped down and glared at her mother while she stirred a packet of artificial sweetener into her tea.

109

"This house is too big for the two of us. And the upkeep is killing me financially. Larry helped me see that it could be an asset and not a liability if I simply sold it and moved."

"Larry!" Carrie exploded. "Since when does he have any say-so in our lives?"

Mrs. Blake shot Carrie a warning glance. "Stop it, Carrie. Larry Farrell is the nicest, most caring man I've ever met. He's only looking out for our best interests."

Carrie snorted disdainfully. "It's not in *my* best interests to move. Where are we supposed to live anyway? Has Larry figured that out too?"

"Don't be fresh. Of course I've thought about it. I'm getting an apartment on the west side. The complex is beautiful and—"

Carrie leapt to her feet. "The west side? But that's out of Martin's school district. I'll have to change schools!"

"You're only starting your sophomore year. You'll have three years to get adjusted to a new high school before you graduate."

"But I want to graduate from Martin."

"Kids switch schools all the time. I don't see what's so special about Martin. It's not even ranked as one of the top high schools in the city."

"But it's *my* school," Carrie wailed. And it was Keith's school and Holly's.

"Well, think about this," her mother argued, her voice rising in pitch. "Living in an apartment will help me save money. And that money will help put you through college." Her mother leaned back in her chair, as if this tidbit was going to be the ultimate persuader.

"Maybe I don't want to go to college," Carrie countered. "Maybe I want to get a job and work after high school."

"And what?" Mrs. Blake snapped. "Be your father's secretary and marry some jerk who can't give you the better things in life? No, I want you to know how to *do* something. You need your own career. Just think what would have happened to us if I hadn't had a career to fall back on."

The truth was, Carrie really did want to go to college, so this tack wasn't getting her anyplace. "Well what about my doctor? And the clinic? They're all on this side of town. And so's support group too."

"You told me you wanted a car. If you have one, I won't have to listen to your father moan about your riding the bus ever again. And there are other doctors and clinics, you know. We can get a recommendation for others—a referral."

"So long as I'm well," Carrie exploded. "But what if I get sick again? What then? I want my regular doctor."

Her mother brushed off Carrie's grim suggestion, stood, scooped up her teacup, and crossed to the sink. "You're perfectly fine, Carrie. Spending a week with that Gardner boy has made you pessimistic. Your cancer's in remission, and it's not going to come back again."

Carrie recalled Keith telling her a similar thing.

What's happened to me won't happen to you, he said. Yet somehow her mother made it sound different. Keith's message had sounded positive, encouraging. Her mother's sounded threatening, as if she was daring Carrie to get sick again. "Nobody knows what's going to happen," she said calmly.

"Well, isn't that just the point?" Her mother's voice had turned conciliatory. "Since we don't know the future, we should enjoy what we have now to the fullest. I have a career—a good one. I have a future and a man in my life who encourages me. I should think you'd be pleased for me."

Carrie felt unsure of what to say. If she said she wasn't pleased, her mother would be hurt. Yet to say she was would be a lie. Her mother came over and put her arm around her. "Maybe I shouldn't have surprised you with the house sale, but Larry knew this realtor, and it all seemed so right. Listen, we'll drive out to the apartment complex next Saturday. You're really going to like it. There's a game room, a sauna, and a pool."

She hugged Carrie, but Carrie found it impossible to respond. "I'm going to Keith's on Saturday."

"Oh. Well, I'm sure you won't be there for the whole day."

"He doesn't have that many 'whole' days left. I'm planning on spending every minute I can with him."

Her mother dropped her arm and walked over and picked up Carrie's suitcase. "We can talk about it later. Right now let's get your things upstairs. Incidentally, the realtor has a key, and I told her to show the house whenever she wants. If you're here alone when she brings a client through, please just stay out of the way."

Wearily Carrie bent and picked up her other bags. Her mother didn't have a buyer for the house yet, and therefore, she had hope that no one would want it. She shook her head skeptically. It was one more miracle she had to hope for.

Carrie went back to work on Monday. She almost asked her dad to stop her mother from selling the house, but he was so busy managing construction projects, she scarcely saw him. Besides, if he did say anything to her, it would probably mean another fight. Bobby was away at camp, and Lynda didn't seem to mind taking her over to Keith's anytime she asked, so Carrie concentrated on her job and her time with Keith and shoved the other stuff out of her mind. It gave her a headache to think about it too much anyway.

At Keith's she met the hospice people. A nurse, Judy, and a social worker, Joy, came to check on him every day. Judy recorded Keith's vital signs—his blood pressure and temperature—and took care of his medical needs. Both women listened to and talked to the family, answering questions and soothing their anxieties. "What happens next?" Mr. Gardner asked. "Is he hurting?" Mrs. Gardner wanted to know. "How much longer will my brother live?" Holly wondered aloud, tearfully.

Because Carrie spent so much time at the house,

and because they treated her as one of the family, she heard them assure the Gardners that Keith wasn't in pain, and that the dying process involved several stages. "His need for food will decrease," Judy explained. "Toward the end he may act confused and may not recognize you." Mrs. Gardner winced when she heard that part. "Also," Joy said, "he'll spend more and more time sleeping and be difficult to arouse. His body will be cool to your touch, and his breathing will become erratic." Carrie really liked the honesty of the hospice people and soon realized that they were there to help the family as much as the patient through the ordeal ahead.

The minister from Keith's church stopped by often, and she found his presence comforting. Twice she ran into visiting kids from the support group. She felt that Keith was nestled in a cocoon of love, and it gave her a sense of peace and acceptance about letting him go. It also helped that family life kept happening all around him, and that there were no IVs, wires, or monitors in his room.

He asked for his study desk to be removed and a lounge chair to be brought in so people could be comfortable when they visited with him. He had his father turn his bed, so that he could look out the window at all times, and he'd asked for a small night table to be placed next to his bed. It held a lamp, his baseball glove, and the terrarium Carrie had given him.

He took pain pills as often as he wanted them. In fact, Mrs. Gardner seemed to be always asking, "Do you hurt, Keith?" and "Can I get you anything to eat?"

Keith was patient, attempting to eat for her sake, but privately he told Carrie, "I'm just not hungry anymore. I mean, my mom's the type who thinks that everything can be fixed with a good meal and a glass of milk." He pulled a Twinkie out from under the covers. "Holly too. Take this, okay? I don't want either one to know I can't force it down."

One afternoon Carrie arrived only to be told that Keith was taking a shower. So she sat next to his bed, waiting for him to finish, feeling grateful that he was having a good day. Jake bounded into the room, saying, "Hi! Did you see how I fixed up the frogs' house?"

She peered into the glass container and saw where he had scooped out one corner and created a pond from an old butter tub. "Do you see the frogs?" he asked impatiently.

The plants had grown thick and lush in the hothouse atmosphere, and at first she could see only the foliage. A philodendron leaf quivered, and finally she saw two miniature frogs crouched beneath it. "Those are from the lake?" she asked. "Why, they've grown into regular, real-live, honest-to-goodness frogs."

Keith came in just then, towel-drying his hair. He wasn't wearing a shirt, and she saw how thin and gaunt he looked. "Jake's quite the frog farmer, huh?"

Jake's face lit up with a smile. "I'm gonna enter 'em in a frog-jumping contest next year at my school. They'll win." He dashed out of the room, and Keith shut the door behind him.

"It's crazy how attached he is to those dumb

frogs," he said. "Don't tell anyone, but so am I. I watch them at night when I can't sleep, and it reminds me of the cabin. And the lake. We had fun, didn't we?"

"The most," she whispered. "I—I wish—" Her voice had grown thick, and she didn't trust it.

He put his fingertips on her lips. "I wish too. But it doesn't change things." His skin and the whites of his eyes had a distinct yellow cast. "It's nice of you to come by every day," he told her, easing down on the bed. "You don't have to, you know."

She picked at the nap of the carpet with the toe of her sandal. "Sure I do. It's a good excuse for leaving work early."

He smiled and pulled on a shirt. "Do you like the job?"

"Dad's out most of the time, and so it's just me and Patty—that's his secretary. She's nice. Her baby was sick last week, so I had to keep things running without her."

"I'll bet you did fine."

"A piece of cake."

"You went in for your lab work too, didn't you?"

It touched her that he could remember such details, especially when he was so sick. "They pronounced me well and fine," she told him.

"I'm glad. I was hoping you'd get a good report. Any buyers for your house?"

"No offers, but lots of people are looking. The realtor says that this is the best time for it to sell because families want to be settled in before the school year begins."

"I'm sorry you won't be going to Martin next year. So's Holly."

Carrie turned her face, because the mere mention of it made her want to cry. "Yeah, that's what she told me," she said. "But she's pretty outgoing. She'll do all right."

"A couple of the guys from the baseball team stopped by yesterday. I could tell they didn't want to be here. I mean, what can they say to me? But I'm glad they came anyway." She figured that he must get lonely, but it *was* tough for kids their age to look death in the face, so she could understand how awkward it must have been for them. "Hella stops by too, not as a nurse, but just as a friend. She's a really great lady. I hope she marries some guy who's worthy of her."

His sentiment surprised her, but then he'd only known happily married people, so naturally he'd think such a feat was possible. He eased back onto the bed, and she saw his eyelids droop. "You're tired," she said. "I should let you sleep."

"I took my pain pills while I was in the bathroom," he explained. "I wish they didn't bum me out so bad. I always seem to be fallin' asleep, and I don't want to sleep."

"Why not?"

"Because I'm afraid I won't wake up." His eyelids closed, and his head lolled to one side. For a moment she held her breath until she heard his breathing coming strong and regular. Slowly she exhaled, pulled a coverlet over him, then bent and kissed him lightly on the cheek and left the room.

Chapter Seventeen

~~~

On the Fourth of July, Carrie accompanied her Dad, Lynda and Bobby to the riverfront where they watched a spectacular display of fireworks launched from barges in the river. Brilliant flashes of red, blue, yellow and green sprayed across the dark sky and rockets whistled, then burst with a bang, showering the night with gold dust. Each bang, pop and roar was followed by a dazzling eruption of color. Carrie covered her ears and glanced toward her father, whose tense expression scared her.

His mouth was set in a grim, hard line, and she saw him wince at the sound of the fireworks. It surprised and puzzled her so much that later, when the two of them were back home, sitting on the back porch eating watermelon, she asked him about it. "Didn't you like the fireworks?"

"Sure," he said, watching Bobby race around the yard with a sparkler held high. "Don't I take you kids every year to watch them?"

"You didn't *look* like you were having a good time. It was like the noise was bugging you."

He hesitated, then said quietly, "It's the sound

the firecrackers make. It always reminds me of sniper fire."

Puzzled, she scrunched her forehead. "What's that?"

"In Vietnam we'd be on patrol, and suddenly the trees would come alive with this popping noise, and we'd hit the dirt. The snipers sat up in the trees and picked us off, and we never even saw them. And as for the rockets, every time one went off, lots of us died." He set his slice of watermelon on the porch railing.

"You never told me about Vietnam before. Why?"

"Isn't much to tell." His voice sounded gruff. "I went right after high school with four of my buddies. It seemed sort of exciting at the time, marching off to war." He shook his head. "It wasn't."

She racked her brain, trying to remember what they'd discussed in American history class about the Vietnam War, but the facts were a fuzzy jumble. "Didn't some guys burn their draft cards?"

"Sure. But I did my duty. I did what was right."

"What was it like?" Carrie asked, fascinated. She'd never thought of her father as having a life before she existed, let alone his having fought in a war.

"Vietnam was a hot, stinking jungle, and I wish we could've blown it into the sea."

"But you didn't get hurt, did you?"

"Five of us went over there, but I was the only one to come back."

"Just you? The others were all killed?"

"Gabe Hunter went to a vet hospital. I went to see him, but I picked the wrong day to go. They'd just amputated both his legs, and as I was walking down the hall, I heard him screaming. He never forgave the doctors for doing that to him. He died later."

Carrie couldn't even swallow. "I-is that why you hate hospitals so much?"

He flicked a watermelon seed over the railing. "Partly. I went to the hospital to see you once when you were diagnosed with leukemia. They said you were having a spinal test."

"Spinal tap," she said, correcting him. "It's how they check the spinal fluid for cancer cells, to see whether it's spreading or not."

"Hearing you say that bothers me, Carrie. You're only fifteen years old. Why should a fifteen-year-old know about that stuff?"

Gently she told him, "Dad, I have leukemia, and I have to know all there is to know about it. Pretending it's not there won't make it go away."

He scowled and continued talking as if he hadn't heard her. "I remember walking down that hallway and standing at the door of the lab. I could see what was going on through that little glass window. You were curled into a ball, and some guy was poking a needle into your back. I heard you scream—" He paused; his eyes were unfocused, as if he were seeing pictures from the past. "But you never moved."

"You can't move," she explained patiently. "And I yelled because it hurt. They tell you to scream if you want."

"I wanted to take that doctor apart," her father said. "I couldn't stand the idea of them hurting you."

He shrugged. "I guess that was why it was so hard for me to visit you in that place. I was scared I might start dismantling it."

His confession stunned her. She'd had no idea he'd felt that way. "But sometimes you have to hurt in order to get better," she told him. "Whenever I'd get really sick from the chemo, so sick that I was barfing up my toenails, I'd tell myself, 'This is awful, but at least the cancer cells are suffering too.'"

"I know that up here." He tapped the side of his temple with his forefinger. "But here"—he tapped his chest—"here it's not so easy."

Carrie felt tears forming in her eyes and sniffed them back. Keith was right; girls were always puddling up the place. She wanted to throw herself in her dad's arms. She wanted to tell him she was all right and that she loved him.

He locked his hands behind his head and tipped back in his chair. "I'm real sorry about Keith. I know he's your friend and all, and I know what it's like to watch friends die. It never makes sense to me why kids have to die. Didn't make sense when it happened to my buddies in Nam, doesn't make sense to me now. It's got an odor about it, you know."

"An odor?"

"Death. It smells rank and nasty. Once you've smelled it, you never forget."

Bobby barreled up onto the porch, demanding more sparklers. Carrie watched her father lean over and light two and hand them to Bobby. "Come on, you guys," the boy demanded. "Let's light some fire-crackers."

Her father fairly leapt out of the chair and onto the lawn. Carrie remembered what Lynda had told her once. *It's hard for him to show his feelings. It's just his way of coping.* She picked up her piece of watermelon, but her eyes never left Bobby and her father as they launched a rocket into the night sky.

By the middle of July, Keith was so weak that he could no longer get out of bed. His pain had increased too, and the pills were no longer effective, so hospice brought in an infusion pump for dispensing Keith's morphine. Carrie thought the small machine looked out of place in Keith's room, but the device was a blessing. An IV line, attached to a tiny needle inserted under his skin, kept a steady flow of the potent painkiller flowing into his body continuously.

As his liver failed, his body bloated, and his skin turned quite yellow. But as hard as it was for Carrie to see him so sick, it was harder not to see him at all. So she went to his house as often as possible and sat next to his bed and talked about anything that popped into her mind.

She noticed that even when he was drugged and unable to converse, he responded to the sound of voices. "Hearing is the last of the senses to fail," Judy explained. "That's why we always talk to patients, and that's also why we watch what we say. Talk positively, about happy things, about how much you care."

Once she stopped by on her way to work and found Mrs. Gardner asleep in the lounge chair beside his bed, holding his hand. The scene caught her heart and stayed with her for a long time. The mother's plump pink fingers wrapped around his frail ones, as if she might somehow keep him alive if she could only hold on tight enough.

Hella came one afternoon, and after visiting with Keith, they left him with his mother and Holly and went out onto the front veranda, where an old-fashioned swing hung from hooks in the wooden ceiling. Carrie pushed off from the floor. The swing swayed, its chain creaking in rhythm with the movement. "He's not doing so good, is he?" she finally asked.

"Not very good at all," Hella confirmed, sending a sickening sensation into Carrie's stomach. She wanted to ask, *How much longer?* but didn't have the courage.

"Being at home *is* better than being in the hospital," Carrie told her. "I didn't think so when Keith first told me about hospice, but now I see that it is."

"Hospice is a wonderful program, but not all families can handle a member dying at home. The Gardners are pretty special."

How well Carrie knew that. Even though her father seemed to understand about dying, he was afraid of it. And as for her mother—well, Carrie was certain now that Faye could never deal with the day-in and day-out process.

"What do you think makes them that way?" she asked.

Hella picked at some chipped paint on the armrest of the swing. "They have an amazing depth of love and respect for one another," Hella said. "That helps. But sometimes, Carrie, parents can love their child a lot and still be unable to face watching him die."

"What do you mean?"

"When a teenager dies, so do his parent's dreams and ambitions for him. That's devastating. A parent makes so many plans around a child, and then to have everything altered by premature death—well, I'm telling you, some parents never recover."

"But if they really love their kid, like the Gardners do—"

Hella interrupted. "Love is a factor, but it's more complicated than that. After years of coping with chronic illness, parents, even good ones, can't deal with it anymore. They just simply run out of energy. If a family isn't especially close-knit, they can't handle watching their teen slip away, beyond their help, beyond medical help, and often in terrible pain. So they sort of abandon him—mostly emotionally, sometimes physically. I've seen it happen many times."

"But that's not fair! How can you stand it when parents leave a kid all alone in the hospital?"

"I try not to judge them, Carrie. Yes, some people make lousy parents, but we don't know how we'll act in a situation until it happens to us. As a nurse I try to give the best care I can if the teen is left to die in the hospital, or all the support I can if he goes into the hospice program."

Carrie stared off into the bright, cloudless sky. She felt incredibly sad, on the brink of crying. It was more than the unfairness of Keith's death. If only she could put it into words. "Keith seems able to accept what's happening to him," she said slowly. "I wish I could."

Hella laid her hand along Carrie's arm. "Keith's an extraordinary young man. He doesn't defy, submit to, or deny his dying. In some ways he's transcended it."

"I don't understand what you mean."

"He grieves and mourns over dying, but he also sees it as a spiritual process. He believes in an afterlife, and that gives him peace and hope. It's helping his family through the worst of it too."

"I—I believe in God," Carrie said, her voice small, because she knew deep down she was pretty angry with God and felt ashamed about it. Keith had told her that God was the head umpire and had a right to call the plays because he could see the whole game. Yet she couldn't figure out why he'd allow someone as wonderful as Keith to die so young.

Hella smiled sweetly. "Oh, Carrie. You're such a unique girl. When you were only eleven and I first met you, I thought you were so mature and practical. On the one hand you never tried to deceive yourself about what was happening to you, but you never gave up hope either. You adjusted to having leukemia, and you coped better than any young person I'd ever nursed."

Carrie knew Hella was telling her something

about her parents' failings. True, she'd seen those failings herself many times, but it hadn't made her life easier. Some things couldn't be changed, not her parents' attitudes, not their divorce, not their feelings about one another. "I'm glad there's something like hospice," she said, picking up the thread of her original thought. "I'm glad there are people who can help people through dying, so they don't have to be scared and alone."

"For me that's what nursing's all about, Carrie. It's *caring*."

Just then Holly came out onto the porch. Her eyes were wide, and her face looked pale and frightened. "Mom wants you to come see Keith," Holly said, her voice quivering. "His breathing is all crazy. Hurry. Please, hurry."

Chapter Eighteen

~

Carrie bolted after Holly and Hella into the house and down the hallway to Keith's room. Mrs. Gardner stood beside his bed, her eyes wide with fear. "His breathing sounds funny," she said. "It stops and starts."

Hella leaned down and listened. Finally she said, "It's apnea, and it may be like this for a while. I know it's scary, but it's part of the process."

Keith's eyes flew open just then, and he looked around the bed at their faces. "Carrie," he said, managing a smile. "Have you been waiting long to see me? Someone should have told me you were here."

He'd obviously forgotten he'd seen her earlier. "Not too long," she said. "And I told them not to wake you."

"Did you come for a guitar lesson?"

"No, just to say hello." It was hard for her not to cry.

"But you've been practicing?"

"Sure," she lied.

"Play something for me. Holly, get my guitar so that Carrie can play. Like at the lake."

She took the instrument from Holly, silently pray-

128

ing that she could make her fingers work on the frets. After a few false starts, she managed to pick out a tune. By the time she finished, Keith had drifted off to sleep again. She put the guitar down and looked toward Hella and Mrs. Gardner, who were talking just outside Keith's room.

"I'm so scared," Mrs. Gardner whispered. "Can't you *do* something? Can't you help him?"

"Maybe you should call Judy at hospice," Hella said. "And your husband too."

To Carrie the advice sounded reassuring. The hospice people were on twenty-four-hour call, and Judy had urged the Gardners to call her anytime Keith's condition concerned them. Mrs. Gardner nodded and went to the kitchen.

Numbly Carrie left Keith's room. In the hall she saw Holly was leaning against the wall, tears brimming in her eyes. "I—I thought it was all over when he started breathing that way," she said.

Carrie led her into her bedroom and closed the door. "Are you all right?"

Holly sat on her bed. "My legs are shaking so bad I can hardly stand up." She flopped backward on the bed and started crying. Carrie reached over and handed her a tissue from the box on the dresser. "I—I'm not gonna make it, Carrie. I'm not gonna be able to get through this."

Carrie didn't know what to tell her, but at last she said, "You'll make it. The others will be looking to you." It sounded incredibly trite. She wasn't sure she was going to make it either.

Holly blew her nose and sat up. "I don't think there's gonna be any miracle," she said miserably. "I've asked and asked, but either God's not listening, or he doesn't care."

"Nothing can convince me that God doesn't care about Keith," Carrie told her. "And as for a miracle, Keith didn't expect one."

"Yeah, but I did."

Carrie's heart was breaking for her. "He told me that even if a miracle happens, people still have to die. He said it happened that way for everyone, and that's just the way things are."

"I know what he believes," Holly said. "That death follows life, and after death, life again. But what about us, Carrie? What about the people who get left behind? What are we supposed to do?" As she spoke, Holly wadded the tissue and tossed it across the room into the wastebasket.

"Maybe that's why we have each other," Carrie said slowly. "Maybe the best we can do during our lives is be here for one another through the bad times."

Holly asked, "Will you always be my friend?" Carrie nodded because she didn't trust her voice. "Even if you have to go to some other high school than Martin?"

"We'll have weekends, and there's always the phone. Plus I'll be driving soon." Carrie let the words out in a rush, hoping that by assuring Holly she'd find some assurance for herself. She felt as if everything

"No, sir." He left, and she sat alone at the table with the remains of the half-eaten dinner, her eyes glancing from place to empty place, feeling very much like a character in an abandoned fairy tale. The doorbell rang, and when no one went to the door, she did. She opened it and stared in surprise. "Mom! What are you doing here?"

Faye smiled, but it looked forced and strained. "After you called, I started thinking that you might need some things—toothbrush, deodorant—personal stuff." She held out a small overnight case.

At any other time Carrie might find her deed thoughtful, but all she felt at the moment was confusion. She took the bag and set it inside the door. She thought about asking her in but decided against it. Her mother didn't belong. Not now. Carrie stepped out onto the porch, closing the front door softly behind her. "Would you like to sit in the swing for a few minutes?" she asked.

Her mother sat, but toward the front edge, her spine stiff. "Are you sure you need to be here, Carrie?" she blurted. "I—I mean after all, the boy's so ill—"

"He's dying, Mom."

"It just doesn't seem right . . . him dying here in his own home."

"I told you about hospice already. No one can do anything for Keith except make him comfortable. Mostly, hospice is here for his family. If it was me—"

"Well, it isn't you," her mother interrupted. "You're fine." Her eyes narrowed, and she stared directly at Carrie. "You are fine, aren't you? They didn't say anything at the clinic you're not telling me, did they?"

"No, Mom. I'm fine."

Faye relaxed, then smoothed her skirt. "Did I tell you? I got a promotion yesterday," she said.

"I'm glad," Carrie replied, not sure what her mother expected her to say.

"Larry says I have a lot of potential with the company. I've come so far since the divorce, you know? I mean here I am in a leading accounting firm with a wonderful man in my life. It doesn't seem real sometimes."

"So except for my cancer, life's great, huh?"

Faye stood, causing the swing to shimmy. She walked to the porch railing and gripped it. "I hate your cancer." The vehemence in her voice almost took Carrie's breath away. "I hate it with everything that's in me. Look how it's messed up all our lives."

"I'm sorry I'm messing up your life, Mom." Carrie said the words so quietly, she wasn't sure her mother could even hear them.

"My mother died from it. And so did my favorite aunt—Nora was her name. I remember how horrible it was for them. They hurt so much, and no one could help them. Not all those doctors in the hospital. No one."

"You never told me that before." Carrie watched her mother's shoulders quivering in the moonlight. She felt panicked suddenly, because she'd never once seen her mother break down. "You should have said something to me."

"Why? What difference would it have made?" Carrie thought of all the times she lay alone in the hospital wishing her mother was with her. "You can't imagine what it's like to live with the fear that someday I could get cancer too," Faye said haltingly.

"We're all afraid, Mom."

Her mother sniffed and turned. "And then to have it happen to one of my children—well, it's not fair. And it's all my fault too. If I hadn't been carrying the genes for it—well, it's a fact that cancer runs in families. I should have been more careful about having a family."

Carrie felt a physical pain in her stomach. If only she'd never been born, then they all could have been spared this hurt. "Your father wanted a family, though, and so I gave up my job and everything just to please him. Then you got sick, and everything changed. But you're doing so well. I'm just *certain* that you're going to be one of the lucky ones to beat the disease." She wiped under her eyes with the tips of her fingers and offered a brave smile. "I don't think I could stand it if I didn't have that hope."

Carrie felt numb all over. Inside the house Keith lay dying, and here on the porch in the moonlight, Carrie felt another kind of death was taking place. All at once she wanted her mother to hold her, as she'd seen Mrs. Gardner hold Keith. She wanted so bad to be cuddled. Her mother said, "I—I guess I should let you go back inside."

"Yeah, I guess so." Carrie stood and edged toward the door. "Um—thanks for bringing my stuff by. I'll call you tomorrow, before I come home."

"Larry's taking me furniture shopping. I thought I'd get a new sofa and chairs for the apartment."

Carrie realized she didn't want to be by herself tomorrow if Keith was gone. "Then I'll go to Dad's, and he can bring me home later."

"I'll get something new and pretty, Carrie. I think moving will make you feel better. It'll help put all this behind you."

"Sure, Mom." Carrie turned and went inside and leaned against the doorjamb in the dimly lit foyer. A wall of tears seemed permanently dammed in the back of her throat. Why didn't her mother understand that buying something new could never erase this night, could never take away the hurt she felt in her heart? Not just for Keith, but for herself too.

Carrie took one last look out the window. Her mother's car was still parked out front, and she could just make out her mother's shape sitting behind the wheel, her face buried in her hands. A part of Carrie wanted to run to her and throw herself into her arms. But then she heard voices from the Gardners' living room and the sounds of crying. Her heart lurched. Without another glance she hurried toward the lighted room.

Chapter Nineteen

⌒～

Carrie entered and saw Keith's family gathered together. Mrs. Gardner was crying uncontrollably, clinging to her husband and saying, "We should call an ambulance! I know if we get him to a hospital, they can help him."

"Judy says they can't, honey."

"But he can't breathe! He—he can't get any air."

Holly was hugging her arms to her shoulders and rocking back and forth. Carrie dropped beside her chair. "What's happening?" she asked.

"Judy says the fluid's building up in Keith's lungs. It's like he's drowning in it."

"This was a mistake," Mrs. Gardner cried. "We never should have kept him here at the house. If only we'd taken him to the hospital instead." She clutched Mr. Gardner's arm. "It's not too late. We could leave right now—"

Huddled on the sofa, April, Gwen, and Jake started to weep more loudly. Jake rushed into his mother's arms and buried his face in her lap. "Don't cry, Mommy. Keith's all right. The lady said he's still alive."

Mrs. Gardner held the five-year-old hard against

her body. Just then Judy came into the room. Her face looked tired, but also gentle. "I put a special medicine patch on Keith to dry up his secretions," she said kindly. "He's breathing more easily now."

Mr. Gardner asked, "Should we call an ambulance and have him taken to the hospital?"

"No hospital can help Keith now." Judy touched Mrs. Gardner's arm as she answered. "Nothing can stop what's happening to your son. But it was his wish—and your wish—to have it happen here in his home in his own bed. You've come so far along this road. I'm here to help you any way that I can, but if you want to take him in, then please do. Only remember, he isn't in any pain—"

"But how do you *know* that?" Mrs. Gardner interrupted. "How can you be sure?"

"He's not restless, he's not moaning, and his morphine levels remain high."

Mrs. Gardner turned tortured eyes toward her family. "What should we do? Tell me, what should we do?"

Holly slid off her chair and crossed the floor on her knees to her mother's side. "I think we should go be with him. All of us together."

"Yes," Judy said softly. "Go talk to him, hold his hand, tell him how much you love him. He'll hear you."

Mrs. Gardner wept silently for a moment longer, but finally she nodded her consent. "I guess you're right." She rose, and Mr. Gardner put his arm around her waist to steady her. They started down the hall, and one by one the others followed, reminding Carrie of baby ducks trying not to be separated.

In Keith's room they took positions around his bed, stations where each could see and touch him. There was a staleness, a stagnation in the air, and she wondered if it was the "smell of death" her father had warned her about. She wanted to fling open windows to chase it away but instead stood woodenly, staring down at his motionless body.

In the glow of the lamp, he looked peaceful. "Hi, son," his father said.

"We love you, Keith," Mrs. Gardner said. Her voice had become strong, and all trace of her former doubt and fear was gone.

Jake leaned over his brother, positioning his ear right above Keith's nose. A moment later his face broke into a grin. "You're tickling me," he said. "It makes me feel fuzzy all over."

April bent down and kissed Keith's cheek, and Gwen held his hand. Mrs. Gardner stroked his cheek and kept saying, "I love you . . . I love you."

For her part, Carrie could only watch. Once she tentatively touched his arm, which felt cool, and so she drew her hand back. Mesmerized, she watched his chest rise and fall, fast, then slow. His breath came in gasps, and she held her own breath, willing his to keep coming. His eyelids fluttered open, and he seemed to be staring straight at her, but then they closed, and she realized that he hadn't seen her at all.

At some point Keith asked for water, and his father held a straw to his lips, but he wouldn't drink from it.

"He can't swallow," Judy told him gently, removing the glass from his hand.

Holly told Keith a silly story, as if she could make him laugh and forget how hard it was for him to breathe air. Jake sang a song about a dog named Bingo. Inwardly Carrie wanted it to be over, then hated herself because once it was over, there would be no going back. Silently she begged, "Please God. Please."

Keith's eyes opened once more. "There's a light," he said. His voice sounded raspy. "See the light. It wants me to come." He stared into a corner of his room. Carrie turned, half expecting to see brightness, but saw instead only a darkened corner.

His family bunched about him even more tightly, and Carrie squeezed herself against the wall. She felt the solid surface of the bedside table pressed into her leg and looked down. The baseball mitt had fallen unnoticed to the floor, and the terrarium was tilted toward the wall. The dark green leaves glowed in the light from the desk lamp. She saw the water-filled plastic butter dish and the small white clusters that floated on the surface. *The frogs' eggs.* She remembered catching them at the lake. No . . . not these. The parents of these. How small they were! How hard to believe that the tiny white spheres would turn into living creatures.

She recalled the squirming tadpoles and the sense of wonder she'd first felt over seeing their legs emerge and tails drop off. "Metamorphosis" her biology teacher had taught her during science class. The changing of one thing into another. Again her eyes returned to Keith's heaving chest as he fought for air. She saw then that he too was undergoing a metamorphosis.

His body had become a prison, and his spirit was struggling to break out. Like the tads' tails, Keith's body would have to drop away in order to release his spirit. There was simply no other way for it to be free. Tears swam in her eyes, causing the terrarium to blur and squiggle. The green foliage danced, and the voices of the parent frogs could be heard, calling, calling.

Carrie pushed farther away from Keith's bed, while his family crowded inward, stroking, touching, exploring with soft touches and softer words. Keith's chest heaved. Once, twice, then stilled. He was gone. He'd stepped beyond the room, beyond them all into a world without time. A place without pain.

On the bed his body, his shell, looked empty and abandoned. Keith's metamorphosis was complete.

Chapter Twenty

Carrie circled her bedroom checking and rechecking the boxes, taping some closed and allowing others to remain open in case there were some last-minute items to throw inside. Funny how her lifetime of belongings could be packed away in a single stack of boxes. Digital numbers on her clock radio glowed six-thirty A.M. She had an hour and a half before her dad and Lynda came with the U-Haul trailer. She shouldn't have gotten up so early, but it had been impossible to sleep.

Outside, a fine September rain fell. She hoped the overcast skies would clear up. The weatherman had said they would, but then, who could trust what the weatherman said?

Her mother appeared in her doorway. "Larry will be here to get me at seven," Faye said. She was fully dressed, and her makeup looked perfect, but Carrie could tell that she hadn't slept much either. "You know I don't plan to be here when you leave with your father." The words were terse, the tone cool and accusatory.

"We've been over it, Mom. You know this is the best thing for us both."

"Going to live with your father is good for *me*? How can you say such a thing?"

Carrie sighed, not wanting to start the day with an argument. "I told you, I want to finish school at Martin."

"So you'd leave your mother for the sake of a crummy school? I don't understand you at all, Carrie."

Carrie wanted to say, *I know*, but there was no point, because she could never make her mother understand. There was no way Carrie could ever explain that her leaving had very little to do with staying at Martin.

"I told you we wouldn't be moving until Christmas break," her mother said, in the pleading voice she used so well to get her way. "You don't have to transfer from Martin until January. The new buyers said they didn't want to move in for another three months."

"Mom, let's not argue." Carrie stooped to tape up a book box.

The front doorbell rang. "That must be Larry," Faye said. "He's early."

"You'd better not keep him waiting."

"I'm sorry you don't like him." Again the accusing tone came through her voice. "He's really a very wonderful man."

"He's right for you, Mom. And moving in with Lynda and Dad is right for me."

Tears shimmered in her mother's eyes, and Carrie almost wavered. "You'll call me tonight?" Faye asked.

"Every night, if you want."

"And the weekends?"

"Whenever you want, I'll come over. Dad says he'll get me a car for my birthday."

Faye's mouth twisted into a sour smile. "He gets his way, after all, doesn't he?"

Carrie started to protest, then decided against it. What was the point? Across the space of the room, she studied her mother. She looked pretty, but tense, like a coiled spring. "I hope you'll be happy, Mom," she whispered, hearing her voice catch, and hating it.

"You too," Faye said. Carrie saw her clench and unclench her hands. "You call me tonight."

"I will."

Carrie listened to her mother's heels click down the stairs, heard her open, then shut, the front door. She heard Larry's car drive away, listening until the sound was washed away by the rain.

Carrie sniffed and sat heavily on her bed, now stripped of its linen. The house seemed lonely as familiar sounds echoed off her empty walls. She kept remembering when she'd first told her mother of her decision to move. It had been following the support-group party she'd thown for Keith two weeks after his funeral.

That day she, Holly, and Hella had decorated the small auditorium at the hospital. The banner they'd hung had read: *Bon Voyage*—good journey. It wasn't exactly right for the occasion, but then there wasn't much in the stores to help celebrate a death. Yet it had been what Keith had wanted.

His mother had baked the cake. She said Keith

wouldn't have wanted his friends eating a store-bought cake with yucky bakery frosting. All the Gardners came, as did Judy and Joy from hospice, and so did most of the personnel from the oncology floor and from the clinic and lab. Dr. Fineman had come, and Carrie could have sworn she'd seen tears in his eyes when he'd toasted Keith with a cup of red punch.

Lynda had brought Bobby too. "Your dad would be here, but they were pouring cement today, and you know he has to be there for that." Carrie believed her. Had it not been for the job, he really would have come. Ever since the Fourth of July, there'd been a difference in their relationship. Maybe it was because they'd talked and some of his fears had been aired. Carrie wasn't sure. She only knew that he treated her differently, more like a grown-up.

The night of the party, Carrie had calmly asked her mother, "What would you do if I got sick again?"

"Oh, that's not going to happen."

"But what if it does? Would you let me enter the hospice program like Keith did?"

Her mother had grimaced. "I don't think I'd like that."

"Then who's going to be with me if I relapse and the doctors can't help me?"

"I'll be with you."

"But you hate hospitals."

Faye dismissed the comment with a flip of her hand. "Honestly, this whole episode with Keith Gardner has made you morbid."

Carrie pressed forward, refusing to let her

mother brush her off. "After I saw how Keith died—and how his family all supported him—well, I understand some things about myself I didn't before."

"Such as?"

"Such as, I need someone who'll support me through whatever happens—living or dying."

"I've always been here for you. It's your father who walked out."

"You both left me."

"That's ridiculous. What are you trying to say?"

Carrie drew in a deep breath, hoping it would inflate her courage. "I'm going to move in with Dad and Lynda. And I'm going to finish high school at Martin High."

The color drained from her mother's face. "But I need you with me."

"You have Larry."

"You've always disliked him. I could tell."

"And your job," Carrie continued, as if her mother hadn't spoken. "You want those things. I'm just in the way." She longed for her mother to tell her differently, to persuade her otherwise.

Faye emptied the contents of her iced-tea glass into the sink, and the ice rattled against the stainless steel. "I won't apologize for liking my life now. I like my job—it makes me feel worthwhile. And I like Larry too. I like traveling and dressing in pretty clothes and going to dinner at nice restaurants. What's wrong with that?"

Carrie knew that nothing was wrong with it, but

there wasn't any room for *her* in that scenario. Especially if she got sick again.

Her mother asked, "What can your father give you that I can't? Besides a car?"

How did Carrie tell her that Dad and Lynda could give her a home and a family, the one thing she wanted most? Not a perfect home. Not a family like Keith's, but still a home. "I want to go to Martin in the fall," Carrie said, sidestepping the issue. No—her mother would never understand how her own fear, her own refusal to face reality, had become an insurmountable barrier between them. "It's what I want, and once we move, I can't go there unless I live in the Martin school district. That means moving in with Dad."

"First Bobby and now you," her mother said, sounding hurt. "I've lost you both. I never wanted things to be this way." She said other things too, but Carrie didn't recall them. If once, only once, her mother had said, "I love you. You're my daughter and I want you with me no matter what." But she hadn't. So the next day Carrie had talked to Lynda and her Dad and they'd said they wanted her to move in as soon as possible.

She'd told her mother that she'd leave after Labor Day, just before the school year started. Faye wasn't happy about it but she hadn't tried to talk her out of it again, until this morning. Yet even then, she hadn't said the things Carrie needed to hear.

Downstairs, the doorbell rang and she hurried to

answer it. Her father stood with Lynda and a guy from his construction crew. "You packed up?" her Dad asked. "Frank is going to help me with the heavy stuff."

"It's ready," Carrie said. Outside, the rain had stopped and Lynda's car with a U-haul trailer attached to it was parked in the driveway.

She led them up the stairs to her room, where Lynda put her arm around Carrie's shoulders and hugged her warmly. "We're so excited about you're living with us. I thought we'd put this furniture in the garage and let you decide what you want to keep and what you want to buy new."

"All right," Carrie said, knowing that her stepmother was trying to make her transition easier. The men worked quickly and Carrie stood against a wall, watching. Her father looked out of place in the house, and although she tried to remember happier times when they'd lived together as a family, she couldn't. She realized there probably hadn't been many, but because she was a child she hadn't known that at the time.

Lynda picked up a small box and headed for the door. Carrie decided she should be helping too and grabbed her duffle bag and Keith's guitar.

"Is that Keith's?" Lynda asked.

"Yes. Holly gave it to me after the funeral. She said Keith wanted me to have it. I signed up to take lessons this fall."

"I know you must miss him," Lynda said gently. Tears welled in Carrie's eyes. "I think of him every day. It's like there's a big hollow place inside me and I can't fill it up."

Her father had returned to the room, and he paused beside her. Awkwardly, his big, strong hand touched her shoulder. "It gets smaller with time," he said, "but it never goes completely away. Sometimes, I think about my buddies who died in Nam, and it's as if I can hear them talking.

"And I remember them the way they looked in high school, not the way they looked during the war. I often think about what they might be doing now if they hadn't died so young." Carrie couldn't ever remember seeing her father so serious and emotional, but she understood his pain.

"That's the way I remember Keith—the way he looked at the picnic or at school, not the way he looked at the end." Carrie wrapped her arms around the guitar and rested her cheek along the neck. Keith's scent seemed embedded in the wood and Carrie started to cry softly.

"That's about it," Frank said from the doorway. "I've locked up the trailer."

Lynda balanced the small box. "I'll just tuck this in the front seat."

"I'll hold this in my lap," Carrie managed to say.

She followed them out to the driveway and climbed into the back seat where she carefully lay the guitar across her knees. Lynda and her Dad got in the front and Frank left in his own car. "Are we ready?" Lynda asked, trying to sound cheerful.

"Ready," Carrie answered, staring out the win-

dow at the house. The car and trailer backed out of the
driveway, and made a wide arc in the quiet street.

Carrie kept her eyes focused on her bedroom
window, thinking that even from the road her old
home looked vacant. Lightly, her fingers pressed into
the steel strings of Keith's guitar and as the car
gathered speed, she watched the house grow smaller
and smaller, until it disappeared altogether.

ABOUT THE AUTHOR

LURLENE MCDANIEL lives in Chattanooga, Tennessee, with her two sons, Sean and Erik. She has been a professional writer for more than twenty years and has written radio and television scripts, promotional and advertising copy, and a magazine column. In recent years she has carved a niche in the children's and young adults' book market with inspirational novels. It was her son Sean's diabetes that inspired her to write about life-altering events.

Lurlene McDaniel's other popular Bantam Starfire books include *Too Young to Die, Goodbye Doesn't Mean Forever, Somewhere Between Life and Death* and *Time to Let Go*.

Lurlene loves to hear from her fans. You can write to her % Bantam Books, 666 Fifth Avenue, New York, NY 10103. If you would like a response, please include a self-addressed stamped envelope.

STARFIRE

Ten-Hankie Reading from
Lurlene McDaniel

☐ 28008-2 **TOO YOUNG TO DIE** $2.95

Sixteen-year-old Melissa Austin thought everything was going just great. Then suddenly she faced devastating news. At first she refuses to accept that she has leukemia. But gradually with the support of her family and especially her best friend Jory Delaney, Melissa finds the courage to face her uncertain future.

☐ 28007-4 **GOODBYE DOESN'T MEAN** $2.95
            FOREVER

Jory is overwhelmed by a sense of loss as she watches her best friend Melissa's health deteriorate. As she grapples with the unfairness of Melissa's illness, can Jory find a way to turn her anger into the hope that Melissa wants her to feel?

DON'T MISS THESE
STARFIRE® BOOKS